ON THE FAR HORIZON

CLINT WESTGARD

Published by Lost Quarter Books
www.lostquarterbooks.com

This edition 2017

Cover image from *The Lookout (1900)* by Albert Bierstadt

ISBN: 978-1-928035-28-2

For Jean and Murray, who both had a great love for a good story.

CONTENTS

RIDERS ON THE STORM

1

They had just entered the long and narrow draw past Sounding Creek when the storm hit. It had been threatening from the moment they left MacAllister's, the sky filled with brooding clouds that seemed even more ominous in the last light of the day. Seeing them, they hurried to reach the valley, in the hopes that it would provide some cover for both them and the cattle they were trailing.

At the very least, Amos thought, as the rain began to spatter his duster, it would keep them from scattering everywhere once the winds and the rain truly hit. Nothing had gone as expected to this point though, and the encroaching darkness and the storm promised only more misery.

If he were a superstitious man, Amos might have thought the omens were against them from the start. Coming down to MacAllister's from the north, where the three of them holed up for two days in Davenport's old sod shack, getting in each others' way and on each others' nerves, they came across a dead cow lying abandoned in the scrub. The coyotes and crows had already been at it for at least a day, the smell of it so putrid the horses shied away. Amos stopped to study it for a moment, out of curiosity more than anything, while Wright and H.S. continued on. There was no evident signs as to the cause of the animal's death, which was not out of ordinary in any way, but he still found it disconcerting for some reason.

The next problem came when they arrived at MacAllister's ranch. The cattle were not around Gillespie's Lake, as H.S. had said they would be, but spread out in the surrounding hills. It would take hours to round them up with just the three of them, though the hills would offer them some cover from anyone who happened to be passing by. H.S. had assured them that was extremely unlikely, with MacAllisters gone to Calgary and their hands all in Lethbridge for a day of drinking and whoring.

There was nothing else for it, other than abandoning the job entirely, but to set to work at rounding the herd up as best they could. They split up and went into the hills, thick with brush and trees. Both horses and men were soon in a lather as the cattle ran them across the countryside. Their swears echoed through the air, which might have been a concern, but they saw no sign of anyone.

It was well into the afternoon by the time they had the herd mostly together and heading out of hills toward the ranch. There they encountered their next challenge, for both the cattle and the horses wanted to stop at the lake to drink.

"Just let them," Amos said as Wright whipped at the cattle, who ignored him, plunging their heads into the water. "They'll go better if we just let them."

Reluctantly the others agreed and they had lunch by the lake in full view of the ranch house and the shacks where the hands lived. It was disconcerting to say the least, and Amos found himself unable to look away from the yard, expecting at any moment to see someone coming toward them, rifle in tow.

"Ain't nobody there man," H.S. said, following his

gaze. "I told you. They're all off in town. Nothing to worry about."

Amos nodded, though he did not feel reassured. Wouldn't they leave somebody behind just to keep an eye on things? To stop the very thing they were attempting to do. Evidently not for, except for the cattle and birds circling and crying around the lake, the day was quiet and nothing stirred at the ranch.

When they were through with lunch they got back on their horses and got the cattle moving again, past the lake and south beyond the ranch. After their rest and water the animals moved easily, settling into a comfortable walk. The three riders all relaxed in their saddles, enjoying the warmth of the afternoon sun.

Amos, though, could not resist a final look back at the ranch. As he stared into the distance he was certain he saw movement beside the ranch house. There and then gone. He stopped his horse to watch for a moment, waiting to see if whatever he had seen would reappear. All was quiet and at a call from Wright he turned his horse around and returned to the herd.

2

What remained of the day passed without event, but because of the problems they had encountered in the morning they were well behind schedule if they wanted to be across the border before morning. That would be impossible now. Worse, the most difficult portion of their journey remained and they would have to complete it in darkness, for the sun was setting quickly now, the light going from the day even faster with the storm gathering overhead.

The draw was hard to navigate in daylight and with the added complications of trailing the cattle and the night, it would be even more perilous. Amos did not think about that now, pressing his hat down more firmly upon his head as the drops began to spatter on them. The wind began to gust as well, almost knocking the horses sideways as they picked their way down into the draw.

Amos felt the urge to hurry the horses and cattle ahead of them on into the draw where they might find a bit of shelter, but he knew it would foolish to go faster than they already were. A flash of lightning sparked to the south and west, illuminating the cattle in spectral colors, followed a short time later by the low rumble of the thunder. That seemed to be a signal of some sort, for the rain began to come in torrents only moments and the wind howled as though possessed by spirits.

The air itself felt charged and wild, as though the storm clouds above were about to spill below and engulf them. The animals were disconcerted by it, Amos' horse jumping about as though there were rattlesnakes at his feet.

"God damn," he said and spurred the horse up to join H.S. who was staring up into the rain at the clouds.

"I hope to hell there's no hail in this," H.S. said to him.

"You think we should stay here in the draw?" Amos said, turning his horse about so that he was looking back the way they had come. "Wait out the storm."

H.S. shrugged, "Could be an idea. Cattle might be easier to handle if we keep them down here. Don't know if we can though."

Amos was about to reply when a bolt of lightning illuminated the sky around them. He waited a moment for the thunder that was to follow, so that he would not have to shout over it along with the rain and wind. As he did so, he glanced from H.S. up the trail to where they had entered the draw and was certain he could see the form of a man in amidst the shadows there. In the instant that he saw the form there was another lightning strike, blindingly bright and nearby, the thunder following atop it almost instantaneously. By the time he opened his eyes again, blinking furiously against the sting from the flash, nothing was visible but the coalescing shadows.

"What is it?" H.S. shouted at him.

Amos shook his head and slapped his horse on the haunch, starting back up the draw. The trail they were on was already a muddy, slippery mess and the horse had to pick its way carefully up the, now precarious, incline. The wind blew the rain directly into his face so that it was impossible to see more than a few feet in front of the horse. When he arrived at the spot where he was certain he had seen the man standing there was no one there, nor was there anyone that he could see in amongst the shrub and trees that dotted the trail. He leaned down from the horse to inspect the ground and could make out a variety of hoof prints, no doubt from their own passage, but nothing else.

He shook his head and returned down the trail, muttering to himself under his breath.

"Seeing things?" H.S. shouted at him when he grew near.

"I guess so," Amos said, telling himself it had just been the play of the shadows in the heavy dusk which, with the hour and the clouds swallowing the sky entire, had now turned to utter darkness. The black was leavened only by the flashes of lightning, which illuminated the valley for the briefest of instants as they flickered across the clouds or to the ground. He pushed it from his thoughts, dwelling now on the growing heaviness of his duster and the spreading damp he could feel beneath. It was going to be a long night after a hard day, but if they could get the cattle across the border it would be well worth it.

The cattle, he could see, had reached the bottom of the draw, where it opened up allowing them to spread out off the trail, which they did immediately, heading for the sparse groupings of trees that littered the valley floor. It was the only shelter available to them and they clung to it as the storm continued to intensify. The three cowboys hunched together under few nearby trees as well, though it only provided meager cover from the rain and wind. They leaned in close to each other so they could hear the others as they yelled over the rumble of the storm.

"I think we gotta keep pushing them on," Wright said. "If not we could spend hours trying to get them out of these trees in the dark."

"They won't wanna go," Amos said.

"They won't wanna go no matter what in this weather. But if we don't go now we might still be here come morning. Don't want that."

Reluctantly, both Amos and H.S. agreed and, after a few more stolen moments of respite beneath the trees, they split up and went to start the cattle out of the draw.

Amos went to the eastern end of the valley, letting the horse pick his way around the buckbrush, as he headed to where a group of five cows with their calves was huddled against the slender trunks of the trees there. The animals were even more reluctant to stray from cover than he had been, so he nearly yelled himself hoarse by the time he had the group started south again.

He slowly picked his way back to the trail as he found where some of the other cows had gathered and forced them on their way. He could see Wright just to the west doing the same each time the storm lit up the sky, but H.S. was too far off into the darkness for the lightning to pierce. The storm was almost directly overhead, the thunder now announcing the lightning bursts, which were so close they felt as though they were scalding his eyes.

Wright stayed to trail the cattle they had started back along the path, while Amos went to help H.S. with those that remained. There had to be another twenty cows with calves left to gather and he had seen no sign of them or of H.S., which was strange, given how narrow the draw was and how bright it became with each blast of lightning. The cattle he found easily enough. They were all huddled together in the largest stand of trees to the west of the trail and they refused to move when he came at them with the horse. He tried yelling, clapping and waving his hands and snapping the reins of the horse, but all his sound and fury was easily drowned out by the surrounding storm.

Giving up at last he descended from his horse and plunged into the trees on foot, waving and slapping at the cattle, sending them out scattering to the south. He nearly lost his horse as the cattle leapt from his path, some combination of the storm, the darting cattle and his own flailing startling the nervous creature. When he had calmed it and climbed back on, he rode around the trees to ensure that there were no cattle left and then turned to see what had become of H.S.

3

He was not worried at first. No doubt some calf or heifer had taken off and H.S. had been forced into a pursuit back along the trail. The problem was trying to locate him in the storm and darkness. Even though there was little ground to cover there were enough trees and brush to obscure a man and a horse easily, especially in this darkness. It was only when he had returned to where they had first entered the draw that Amos started to wonder if something had gone wrong. There seemed little chance that a stray calf could have taken him this far.

Amos decided to retrace his steps, going even more slowly to ensure he did not miss anything. Even then he only noticed the body after the horse had shied away from it as they skirted a stand of willow trees. He leapt down to the ground, calling to H.S., certain that he had been thrown and had broke something while chasing after a stray calf. There was no response and, as Amos knelt over H.S., he saw that his eyes were closed and the expression on his face was slack, as if he had fallen asleep where he lay. Amos pressed a hand against his friend's chest to see if a heartbeat remained and his fingers came away sticky and warm.

Though he already knew, Amos held his hand up in front of his eyes, waiting for the next flash of lightning to reveal what was there. When it came he saw plainly the blood being washed clean by the storm. The worst confirmed, he returned his hand to H.S.'s chest, prodding until he found the bullet hole just to the left of his heart. He shivered at the sensation of his finger descending within his friend's body and quickly pulled his hand free, returning a moment later to search his belongings. H.S.'s wallet was still there and Amos took it, along with the belt that held his pistol and bullets.

The overwhelming feeling of being watched seized him as crouched raiding the dead, though he told himself that was just his own guilt working at him. If whoever had done this was near enough to see him to shoot, and he would have had to be very close to manage such a shot in this storm, he would be dead already. Still, Amos did not linger, knowing he needed to find Wright and warn him. They would have to be on watch now, a difficult task given the darkness and the weather. He did not want to think about what would happen once they were out of the draw trying to herd the cattle with just the two of them, to say nothing of specter of a pursuer on their trail.

The shadows seemed ominous as Amos made his way back along the trail, hurrying the stragglers up to the main herd where Wright awaited him. Every time a bolt of lightning crashed down, sending colors reverberating through his eyes, he imagined he saw a man crouched and slowly taking aim with a gun from above the draw. He met Wright coming back up the trail, looking miserable and drawn.

"Where the hell is H.S.?" Wright said, his voice sounding thin and strained over the tumult of the storm. "I've been having a hell of time up here."

Amos leaned over to yell in his ear about what he had discovered.

"God damn," Wright said. "Are you sure?"

Amos handed him the belt with H.S.'s pistol. Wright looked at it, fingering the holster and shaking his head and then stared off into the storm.

Amos grabbed his friend's shoulder. "Come on," he said, "We gotta get outta here. Whoever did this is still here. We need to get out of the draw into the open where they can't hide."

"Who the hell could it be?" Wright said.

"Does it matter? Maybe there was somebody still at MacAllisters."

"No," Wright said. "No. H.S. said there was nobody. He said."

Amos didn't reply and slapped his horse, which leapt forward. The cattle nearest him were startled and he let out a whoop to get them running. Wright joined him a moment later, both of them shouting and pushing the cattle forward as fast as they could. Amos found himself constantly checking over his shoulder at the trees, where he was certain someone lay hidden in wait watching them, waiting for the right moment to strike.

To calm his jangled nerves he tried to reason through who they might be dealing with. In spite of Wright's insistence otherwise, it seemed most likely to Amos that this was someone from MacAllisters, someone who had stayed behind rather than head into Lethbridge. Given that H.S. had only been attacked once he had moved out of their sight, it stood to reason that there was only one man unwilling to risk a direct confrontation. Which meant that, so long as they stayed together in the draw, they would be fine. Once they were out of the valley and onto the prairie the man following them would be as exposed as they were.

If they had any luck at all the storm would be past them by then as well, but for now it seemed to be intensifying again after a brief lull. One blast of lightning sparked a dozen more, the thunder exploding and echoing in a demented symphony. It came with such fury and was so near them, just in the hills above the draw, that they could feel the charge in the air and smell the lightning. The cattle seemed spooked by it and took off at a dead run out of the valley, Amos and Wright on their heels.

As they emerged from the narrow path to the broad swath of prairie above the draw, the cattle spread in several directions at once, trying to race the storm. Amos and Wright came behind, swearing at their bad luck, Amos going to the east and Wright to the west, trying to bring the herd back together before they were scattered to the winds. All the while, as he slapped at his horse and urged it on, Amos thought of the man behind them in his own pursuit who had his choice of prey now.

He couldn't worry about that now, he had to focus on the task at hand or everything would be lost. There was still money to be made here after all, if they could just make it through the night and across the border to market. It was impossible to make out where he was going and where the cattle were, the darkness near absolute but for when a blast of lightning would land and make visible the plain they were now upon. The wind was fiercer away from the shelter of the valley, the rain cutting into his face, making it hard to keep his eyes open for those brief moments of illumination.

A group of heifers, perhaps five, had opened a lead on the rest and were veering further east by the moment. He knew that if he could manage to slow them down and get them turned the rest of those scattered behind would follow suit. At least they would if the circumstances were normal. The storm though, complicated everything. The cattle might not even have a sense of where the rest of the herd was, they might think they were alone. Amos urged his horse on, hoping it could see their way better than he. It made no difference, he could not seem to gain on the cattle, no matter how fast the horse galloped. Why, he thought, was everything going wrong?

He was about to give up, to pull up the horse before it grew lame or exhausted, but the next flash of lightning showed the cattle nearer so he pressed on. Each moment drew them closer, their effort flagging. He drew alongside the lead cow and with whoops and calls began to guide her back to where he assumed the rest of the herd now was. The cattle slowed from their run to a trot, tongues lathered and hanging out from exhaustion and thirst. Amos let out a shout of triumph and eased his horse into a lope.

4

He caught sight of Wright during one of the storms intermittent flashes. He had gained control of the rest of the stampeding cattle and was angling them to the south. The cattle Amos was trailing picked up their pace as they caught sight of their companions and he slapped his thigh in delight. They had done it, facing disaster they had turned it aside and now, if they could just survive this storm and the night, they would be fine. He raised a hand to salute Wright when the sky was next sent alight, wanting to share this feeling. This was what it was, he thought, to be alive. To have faced death and ruin and come through the other side unscathed.

Wright did not see him, he was turned away when the next flash of lightning lanced across the sky, frowning at something behind him. Amos could not see what he might have been looking at, the darkness still holding firm in the far distance. It did not matter, it could only mean one thing. He urged his horse into a gallop again, knowing that time was of the essence now, reaching to his side for the pistol at his belt.

Darkness seemed to swallow the whole prairie, only tiny flickers illuminating the distant and dark clouds, the thunder sounding far away. Amos cursed this sudden shift in the storm, coming as it had at the worst possible moment. He tried to aim himself in the direction where he thought he had last seen Wright. In his mind's eye he could still see that last image, captured in that instant of jagged light, of Wright looking back at their unseen pursuer.

Amos rode until he was certain that he had gone too far, passing the point where he had last seen Wright and then angled his horse south. He could hear the cows ahead calling to their calves, so he knew that Wright must be nearby, unless the worst had happened as he feared. It was that fear that kept him silent as he went ahead, his heart racing, his stomach as unsettled as the sky above.

He had just begun to worry that he might wander in the darkness for hours without finding any trace of Wright, when his horse whinnied and another responded nearby. He let his reins go slack, allowing the animals to find each other. When they were near enough that he could make out the form of the other horse he leaned over and peered at its saddle and the pack it was carrying and was able to see enough to confirm whose it was. He sat rigidly on his own animal, unable to think, seeing only that last image of Wright replaying again and again in his mind.

The rain had fallen to a drizzle and there had been no further lightning strikes for some time. The storm was passing, which meant that he would have the darkness to protect him as he trailed the cattle south. How he proposed to do that, one man with fifty head of cattle on the open range, he could not say, but it was the only thought that got him moving again. He reached over and took the reins of Wright's horse, thinking that, if the cattle proved too difficult to move, he would at least have it to sell.

As he started forward the horse would not budge, even after he yanked hard on the reins. Confused, he turned back to see what the problem was, peering through the shadows at the agitated animal. As he stared it slowly dawned on him that the horse was hobbled. Why would Wright have bothered with that, he wondered? The realization came a moment later, in the same instant the gunshot rang out and bullet hissed past his face, near enough that he could feel its heat.

The shot startled his horse which jumped forward, bucking and twisting violently, sending Amos flying from its back. He landed hard on the ground, knocking the air from his chest. As he tried to recover his breath, he reached for his gun only to find an empty holster. The gun had been in his hand, he recalled dimly through his agony. Panic seized him and he forced himself to crawl away from where he lay, knowing that whoever was out there would be looking for him.

The night was his only aide as he crouched on the ground, hoping his labored breathing did not mark him for the shooter. His knee ached and when he finally managed to get to his feet he found he could barely put any weight on it. His only chance, he knew, was to find his horse wherever it was in the darkness and hope to outrun whoever was after him. After scrambling and slipping about on the rain-soaked ground for a few panic-stricken moments, he realized that it would be far easier to return to Wright's horse. His attacker would expect him to flee and, with the darkness, might not even know that he had been thrown after his shot. He could only hope.

He crept back towards the hobbled horse, staying low to the ground, in case his assailant heard him and decided to let off a blind shot. The horse was still there, standing quietly, much to his relief, as he stroked its side and loosened the hobbles about its feet. That done, he hoisted himself into the saddle, ducking down and matching his form to the horse's as much as possible. After some brief fumbling he managed to gather the reins into his hands and started the horse forward. With each step the horse took he was certain a gunshot would follow, but none did.

At last, deciding that he had escaped notice, he spurred the horse hard and went off at a gallop to the west, abandoning the stolen cattle. Whichever one of the

MacAllisters, or their people, was after him, would hopefully be more concerned with getting their cattle back than pursuing vengeance against him. And, if not, the foothills were a mile or two away. He thought he had reasonable chance of losing any pursuit in the darkness there. At the very least, he could find somewhere to hide for the rest of the night.

He heard nothing but the pounding of the horse's hoofs on the prairie, the storm now almost dissipated as it passed east. A slight glimmer of light had begun to show on horizon behind him, the first sign of the coming dawn. If morning came and he was still on the open prairie...the thought was best left unfinished. He leaned down so that his cheek was pressed against the horse's neck.

The lightning, when it came, was a shock, for the sky above was clear but for a few blots of cloud. None appeared to be near him, the storm now to the east, though he knew that could be a trick of perspective. The bolt was so near that for an instant he believed that it had struck him. The hair on neck and arms was standing on end, soaked as it was. The horse continued to churn its feet beneath him, even as the thunder resounded around them, a deafening cacophony that made his ears feel like they were about to explode. As the moment passed he was filled again with elation, to have passed so near to death and to thwart it.

He wanted to laugh aloud, but didn't dare. A warmth began to spread along his chest as a tickle of pain, hidden beneath the dull ache of his knee, became a sharp agony that obliterated all other feeling. He slipped his hand within his duster and looked down disbelieving when it came away damp and warm. There was no shot, he thought in disbelief. He was still puzzling through this conundrum when he slid from the horse and fell to the ground, unmoving, as it ran on, disappearing into the night.

HART'S CROSSING

I DON'T RECALL the exact details of my return to Hart's Crossing. It was after the accident, that much is certain, but beyond that nothing is. My memory is troubled, whether from that incident, or some other that followed. This uncertainty worries me, on the occasions when my thoughts drift to those days, though I try not to allow them to. That is a futile struggle when I find myself unable to leave Hart's Crossing. So much of the past is still alive for me in this place, for it cannot die.

Hart's Crossing was once my home, a place where I loved and was loved in return, but no longer. Now it is my prison, a place where it seems I am doomed to remain for all the time that is left to me, embittered against my captors and hated and feared by them in equal measure. Such a cruel twist of fate that it should come to this end, after such a beautiful beginning. I cannot account for it, but then my memory, since the accident, is not what it was.

My days now are spent hiding from those I once welcomed with laughter and delight. I lurk in the bedrooms when everyone else is downstairs taking their meals, or whiling away an evening at cards. Only at night, when they are asleep, do I dare to descend, stalking the parlor and the kitchen like a cat after a mouse. Sometimes the floors creak at my passage, or I brush against some book sending it to the floor, announcing my presence for all to hear. In those moments I flee to the cellar or the attic, if I am able, and remain until they leave me in peace.

But there can be little solace here for me. No longer. Why do I remain then? It is hard for me to explain, but I shall try.

I came to Hart's Crossing three years ago, a girl of no more than fourteen. My father had died suddenly of a hidden ailment in his heart, according to the doctor who examined him. My mother had passed of tuberculosis not long after I was born. My father's sister, Muriel, who I had never met, sent for me to come live with her. She had settled with her husband in the Northwest Territories. His name was Andrew Hart and he was a well-to-do rancher, living in the foothills west of a growing town called Calgary.

Having no other family to call my own, I undertook the long journey from Port Arthur, traveling with all the belongings I could claim as my own in a single matchbox case. My father had left me little—having little to begin with—and so I needed to rely on the kindness of these relative strangers if I was to hope to survive. My journey was one of relative boredom, watching the unvarying prairie countryside pass from train car, relieved only by fear at what awaited me at journey's end.

My aunt met me Calgary at the station. She was much younger than my mother, not much older than me, in fact, and, as many would soon comment, we looked as though we were sisters. She treated me as a sister from the first, taking me into her arms and welcoming me warmly. A carriage was waiting for us, and a ranch hand loaded my meager belongings, while Muriel told me all there was to know of Hart's Crossing.

It was named after her husband, a man as stern and forbidding, as Muriel was inviting and kind. Hart's Crossing was what everyone called his ranch house, for, as Muriel told me, it was near a crossing of the Elbow River which everyone in those parts used. The house itself was vast beyond my imagination, just as were the mountains I could see to the west. Mr. Hart and Muriel had a young son Andy, of no more than two years. There was also an elder son, of an age with Muriel, from an earlier marriage, by the name of Jonathan, though everyone called him Jack.

I settled into my new home rather easily thanks to Muriel and Jack, who was a charmer with a smile that took my breath away. Mr. Hart and I exchanged only a few brief pleasantries upon my arrival, otherwise he was distant and preoccupied, seeming not to notice that I, or indeed his wife and children, were present. I helped out as best I could in my new home, caring for young Andy and assisting Muriel in her chores, and tried to be happy in this new home that did not feel it.

Since my accident I suffer from bouts of confusion, absences where my thoughts go somewhere else and return without any apparent reason. It is hard to describe the absences, except to say they are exactly that. My whole being, body and soul, vanishes for a time, only to return here to this house. Where it goes I cannot say. It is like a vast emptiness, filled with darkness, overcomes my senses. But I do have the distinct sense of going and then returning.

The emptiness holds no fear for me, in spite of the darkness and the absence. Hart's Crossing is what terrifies me. Each day I stay my fear and worry grows, until it feels like I cannot hold any more within me. The absences, as disorienting as they are, seem welcome distractions. I long to escape to the emptiness, whatever it is, even if the darkness and nothing is all that is to be found there. It would be better than to stay here in this house where so many terrible things have taken place.

It was in the early months of my stay at Hart's Crossing that I grew to fear Andrew Hart. At first he seemed merely reserved and intimidating, as many of the men I have had the occasion to know are. They all made me timid and a little frightened, but ultimately I knew they meant no harm, in spite of their taciturn inclinations. With Mr. Hart it was different. His general attitude, the way he narrowed his eyes when he saw me, or his carefully parsed words that he delivered like blows, began to seem somehow sinister.

I cannot say what it was that led me to such a belief. Nothing changed in what he did. He continued to, for all intents and purposes, ignore my existence entirely. The only words we exchanged were the most banal of pleasantries, only what politeness demanded and not a sentence more. For my part, I avoided him as best I could, engineering things so that we were never alone in the same room.

It was something about the way he watched me when he believed no one was observing him. There was some aspect about his expression in those moments that disturbed me deeply, as though I was seeing the real man then. It would be there and gone, his habitual distant expression returning as soon as he felt my gaze upon his. Whatever had been there vanished, gone so quickly I found myself wondering if I had only imagined it.

I do not know if anyone else every noticed these glimpses of the true man, as I came to believe, but I became all too aware of them. Every time we shared a room, I was always conscious of where Mr. Hart was and what he was doing. As soon as he turned his gaze upon me I felt it. Sometimes I felt daring enough to turn and meet his eyes, letting him know that I knew he was observing me and I did not approve of it. Mostly I suffered under his watch, too frightened of the man to do anything about it.

I thought of telling Muriel about it, but that seemed impossible. How does one tell one's aunt that her husband might harbor unnatural desires for her niece? Who knew how she would react, or how Mr. Hart would if she confronted him about it. I had no money and no other place in the world to go. I needed to stay in both their good graces, at least until I was old enough and had the means to make my own way in the world.

One day, over a year into my stay in Hart's Crossing, my worst fears were realized and I found myself alone with Mr. Hart. I do not recall where Jack or Muriel were, but both of them were absent. Andy was having a nap in his room and so I had come downstairs to the parlor to read a little. Even Felicia, the girl who helped out with the cooking and cleaning, was gone, out in the yard doing some chores, so I was expecting to see her when the door opened and Mr. Hart stepped inside. He had said he was going to Calgary at lunch and would not be back until the next morning, so I was utterly shocked to see him.

He too seemed uncertain when he stepped from entryway into the parlor, pausing on the threshold, his expression, unreadable before coming to stand before me. "Where's the boy?" he said in a gruff voice, without preamble.

I swallowed, feeling the color drain from face and set my book down upon my lap. "He's taking a nap in his room. Would you like me to wake him?"

Mr. Hart shook his head. "No, that won't be necessary. Thank you. Everyone else is gone, are they?"

"Yes," I said, my voice and hands trembling. "I don't know where they've gotten to."

Mr. Hart nodded and looked away, before turning his intense eyes upon me once again. His eyes narrowed, as though he were trying to judge whether what I was saying was true. I was unable to bear the scrutiny and had to look away.

"I thought you were going to Calgary for the day," I

said, hoping to distract him from whatever was on his mind.

He blinked in surprise. "Oh, yes. I was. Some other matter came up. I'll go tomorrow. My business there can wait."

"Of course," I said, taking my book in my hands again in the hopes that this would be the end of our conversation and my intense discomfort.

Instead Mr. Hart sat in the chair across from me, leaning upon one arm and putting a hand underneath his chin. "We have not had occasion to speak much, you and I," he said, with a false kindness I found off-putting.

"No," I said, in a quiet voice, taking up an intense study of the floor.

He paused and I could feel him looking me up and down with his eyes. "You look remarkably like your aunt, you know. You could be sisters."

"Yes," I said, wishing desperately I could float away and disappear like a spirit upon the wind.

"Yet your manner could not be more different." I risked a quick glance up from the floor and was met by an awkward, lopsided smile and looked away again, my face going flush. "You are the very model of womanhood," he said. "Demure and obedient. Kind. Don't think I haven't noticed the way you treat the boy. This household is unequivocally better with you in it, I must say. I'm glad you'll be with us for the foreseeable future."

The way he said the last felt to me as though he were announcing a sentence of punishment for wrongs I had committed. I forced a smile to my face and met his unsettling eyes. "Thank you," I said with no feeling.

Mr. Hart nodded, as though I had responded correctly. "I admit I have neglected to get to know you the past year and, as you're going to be a member of this household, I would like to rectify that matter. I'm going to suggest we conduct a weekly chat—nothing too rigorous, just whatever the moment suggests to us, so that I might get the measure of you a little better."

I could not seem to move or speak so much as a word, sweat collecting on the back of my dress, at the thought of these weekly talks with this awful man. There was no way I could see to deny him what he wanted, no matter how much I fervently wished.

"There is also the matter of your eventual marriage to think of," he added. He paused and seemed ready to say something else, before abruptly rising to his feet and leaving the parlor without so much as a word or acknowledgment.

I picked up my book to read again, but the words before me were all a blur. All I could think of was what might await me in my private conferences with Mr. Hart and the thought left me ill.

Young Andy is playing in his room and I stop to listen for a time, lurking just outside his door. Though I try to avoid the others, I cannot stay away from him for long. He is so innocent still, his thoughts untrammeled by any of the ills that beset this place. The dangers that lurk in the shadows of Hart's Crossing are unknown to him. How I wish it could stay so for him. In the end he shall be consumed by it, as I was, or perhaps he will become one with it. I don't know which I fear more.

Felicia, is there with him, keeping him company as I used to. The delight he takes in her jokes and stories pains me, for that pleasure used to be mine. Now I am cast out from that welcome circle, unable to take part in it, though I am so near.

"Where is Alice?" Andy asks, a dagger to my heart.

Felicia pauses, uncertain how to proceed. "She's still here. You know we talked about that. And she loves you very much."

"But I want to play with her."

My eyes sting with tears that do not come. I have no crying left in me.

"I know. We all want her to, but that's not possible anymore. Remember."

"Because of the accident."

"Yes."

I move on down the hall, unable to bear hearing any more.

"Did you hear something?" Felicia says, a tremor of fear that she is unable to hide cutting through her voice.

I do not hear the rest. I go downstairs, determined to leave Hart's Crossing this time for good. There is only pain here, and memories that become more bitter than sweet the longer I remain. But, as is always the case, I am brought face to face with the reality of my situation. I am unable to leave and, even if I could, I have nowhere to go.

My private conferences with Mr. Hart proved to be more awkward and odd than threatening. He made no attempt upon my virtue, and in fact seemed entirely uninterested in me. His attention lay on the happenings of the house while he was absent. Despite my reservations and loathing for the man, I told Mr. Hart what I observed of everyone. I felt I had little choice in the matter and it all seemed harmless enough to me. What did Jack and Muriel have to hide from their father and husband? Andy was but a child and Felicia little more than that, though she already kept the house. Surely their day to day lives were of no consequence to Mr. Hart either. Yet it was clear he harbored suspicions against someone in Hart's Crossing, though he was very careful not to reveal his thoughts to me in any of our conferences, showing no reaction to anything I said.

It was Jack who at last revealed the truth to me some months later. Everyone, even Muriel, had pretended that the weekly conferences Mr. Hart held with me were what he claimed: an effort on his part to get to know me better in the hopes of finding me a suitable husband. That Mr. Hart was using me as his spy upon them was something they all studiously ignored, for which I was glad. It would be an extremely embarrassing thing to be forced to admit and I hated that I felt compelled to do it and was grateful that everyone simply acted as though nothing untoward was going on.

Jack invited me to come with him on a trip into Gleneagle, the nearest village to Hart's Crossing, where he had some business to attend to. I leapt at his offer, excited at the opportunity to get out of Hart's Crossing for the day, even if it was just to a town a couple of miles away, and the chance to spend some time alone with Jack. Such opportunities were rare for me, though I longed for more.

The trip into town and our stay there was uneventful. Jack was wonderful companion, full of jokes and stories that only made me like him all the more. The day passed in a delightful blur. It was only as Jack set the horse and buggy on the road back to Hart's Crossing that he grew serious and turned to me.

"How do you enjoy being my father's spy?"

My heart broke at his words and I wanted to weep. I flushed bright red and stammered out something halfway between an apology and a denial.

He laughed. "No need to pretend, I know exactly what your weekly meetings are about. Don't worry, I don't mind. If it keeps father's peace of mind, all the better. He's very suspicious, you know. Has he told you anything about why he's asking you all these questions?"

"No," I said hurriedly, my heart still hammering with fear. "All he does is ask me what has happened in the house that week."

"And you tell him? Everything?" Jack said, glancing at me sidelong.

I nodded. "Yes. I…I just didn't know what else to do when he started asking me. And it seemed harmless enough. I mean there's nothing that goes on that's worth mentioning really."

"Indeed," Jack said, seeming relieved. "But my father

has always had a suspicious nature, I'm afraid. It's only grown worse since Muriel arrived and young Andy was born."

I studied him from across the buggy seat, while he looked ahead watching the horse as it made its steady way down the road. "Why would that make him more suspicious?" I said, thinking of poor Muriel.

"Oh, he's worried about me, you see. He's never much cared for me. There's no denying it, it's the truth," he said, over my protests. "But I was the one who was going to inherit Hart's Crossing. His legacy. There was no one else. Until Andy was born, that is."

"You think he will give Hart's Crossing to Andy?" I said, unable to quite believe it. I had always assumed it would be Jack who would take over for his father. Why else was he staying at Hart's Crossing and doing the work that he was doing, if he didn't expect to get at least a part in the operations?

"Maybe. Maybe not. I don't much care, frankly," Jack said with a shrug. "If he wants it to go to Andy, so be it. But he thinks I'm conniving against Andy and Muriel and him. I don't know how I could even. It's not as though I can change his will. Not that I even know what's in it."

I just nodded, not venturing to say anything, unsure what to make of his casual dismissal of a fraught relationship with his father.

Jack looked at me and smiled. "Anyway, none of that concerns you in any way, so no sense in worrying about it. Whatever is between father and me will sort itself out. You've got no part in it. And I've got nothing to hide, so you can go right on telling him what's happening. It won't change a damn thing."

"Maybe it will help," I ventured halfheartedly.

Jack shook his head. "No. Father's got it in his head that I'm up to no good. No matter what you tell him, he'll just see it as more proof that I'm conspiring against him. It's just what he is."

We rode in silence down the road, both of us mulling our thoughts and listening to the rhythmic clop of the horse's hooves and the steady turning of the buggy's wheels. I was still uncertain about what to take from our conversation. For all his casualness, and the blitheness with which he waved aside his differences with his father, I sensed that Jack had intended to have this conversation with me. That had been the reason behind his invitation to me to join him today. If that was the case, what had he hoped to gain from it? It could not just be to let me know that he was unconcerned with me being his father's spy.

As if he sensed my questions, he said, "I'm glad we go the chance to spend today together."

"Me too," I said, my voice quiet, waiting for what he was going to say next.

"I'm just sorry we had to talk about this. It's an ugly thing. I didn't want it to touch you, but it has unfortunately. So I just want you to know that it doesn't change anything. You can tell my father whatever you like. I've nothing to hide, as I said. And it won't change our friendship. I want you to understand I care for you a great deal Alice."

I looked at him sharply, my heart soaring, even as I told myself not to let my hopes cloud my judgment. He smiled at me and put a hand on mine, not saying anything more. I went still, hardly daring to breath, and leaned against him on the buggy seat, feeling his warmth touching mine. We sat like that the rest of the way home.

At night I sometimes stand upon the veranda of Hart's Crossing and look out upon the dark sky and the multitude of stars there, wishing I could traverse those impassible distances, while the rest of the house slumbers. I can hear the horses stirring in the barn and I imagine myself harnessing them to one of the buggies and letting them carry me away. Those are cruel dreams and I don't know why I allow them to haunt me, when there is nothing I can do to realize them.

This night, as I listen to the horses and watch the stars, letting them torture me yet again, I suddenly realize I am not alone. Andrew Hart has joined me on the veranda. He paces before me, seeming not to notice me in the darkness and I drift back to the where night is deepest, as far away as I can get while still observing him. Like a man possessed he walks back and forth, traversing the same path, never once looking up, least of all in my direction.

He begins to mutter to himself under his breath as he paces, shaking his head at his interjections. "Bloody idiots. All of them. Do they think me a fool? Do they think I don't know what has happened here?"

His manner and his voice are so unlike the man who held his conferences with me. That Andrew Hart never betrayed his true feelings, keeping himself at a careful remove. This Andrew Hart is anguished, torn apart by emotion, nearly unrecognizable.

"That poor girl. She did not deserve this. Bloody Jack should have left well enough alone. But he thought he was so clever."

He stops still, going rigid, his words dying in his mouth. He looks around, peering in my direction, as though he has heard something. But he does not see me through the darkness and he resumes his pacing. No one ever does.

Jack courted me in secret over the next year, insisting that we keep our feelings for each other hidden from the rest of Hart's Crossing. It was for my own protection, he said, and, though it stung me, I could see the logic in it. Mr. Hart was unpredictable in his passions, according to Jack, and if he thought I was in league with his son against him, he might banish me from his house. That was something I could neither afford nor bear to contemplate, given my growing affections for Jack.

He was forever kind, forever apologetic about the

situation we were trapped in as a result of his poor relations with his father. We had little time to ourselves, for the house was rarely empty, and there were few excuses we could find to be together alone. There were stolen glances and embraces when we though no one was looking, but otherwise we said nothing about our burgeoning love to anyone. Muriel suspected, I think, for at times I would forget myself and stare at Jack, only to find her looking at me, a curious smile on her face.

I longed to share my secret with her, though Jack warned me against it. "My father might turn on her if he suspects she knew and kept this secret from him. I don't want any harm to come to her either."

We were talking on another of our journeys to Gleneagle, which Jack had made a regular occurrence to give us some time to ourselves. Our trips had aroused Mr. Hart's suspicions, but I allayed them by saying that I accompanied Jack because I enjoyed the chance to be away from Hart's Crossing and meet new people. This seemed to mollify him, for he knew that Jack had things to take care of in Gleneagle, and I was careful to only relate the most innocuous of anecdotes about our sojourns.

"Why don't we just leave Hart's Crossing?" I said, giving voice to a question that had been in my head for months, but which I had not dared give voice to. "You say you don't care about the ranch. There's nothing else for you here. There's nothing for me either. We could go somewhere and start our own lives."

Jack swallowed and looked at me, a sad smile on his face. "I can't do it," he said. "I can't leave this place. I know I said that I don't care about whether Andy gets Hart's Crossing or me, and it's true. I don't. But I do care about what happens to it. I want to make sure that it's in good hands. I don't expect you to understand."

"No. I do," I said, trying not to let my disappointment show.

"Don't worry," he said to me. "Our time will come.

You'll see."

But the weeks and months went on, with nothing changing except that my yearning for Jack grew until it was nearly beyond my control. It made me miserable that we could not be together, that our love had to stay hidden from everyone, and that my affections had to remain unrequited. We had shared only a few stolen and hurried kisses while on the road to or from Gleneagle and I wanted so much more.

I began to resent Mr. Hart and his interminable prying conferences, so much so that I could barely hide it. He was the one who hated Jack and was keeping us apart. My replies to his questions became curt and halfhearted. I even rolled my eyes a time or two. He seemed not to notice, or, if he did, only ascribed it to my willful feminine nature. Regardless, he offered no comment on my change in attitude, continuing with his inquiries as though nothing had changed.

It was Muriel who confronted me about my obvious misery one day as we hung the laundry on the line behind the house. "What has gotten into you these last months?" she said, speaking around a clothespin in her mouth. "I hope you aren't unhappy here."

"No," I said, a little too quickly. "I couldn't be happier to be here. And I'm so thankful to you and Mr. Hart, for all the kindness you've shown me."

But Muriel would not relent, continuing to ask me what was wrong until I at last gave in and told her about Jack's and my secret love. I expected her to be happy for me— she knew Jack was a good and kind man, after all—but she was taken aback by my revelation. She went very still and would not say anything for a time, her expression unreadable. Her reaction was so unexpected it frightened me, leading me to wonder if I had done something wrong.

Muriel spoke in a monotone, though her voice was heavy with undercurrents of feeling. "You love him? Are you certain?"

"Yes," I said, desperate now to convince her that this romance was as wondrous as I felt it was. "And he loves me. I've never felt this way about someone before."

"Jack is charming," Muriel said, though she seemed to be talking to herself. "I'd hoped you wouldn't get involved in all this…these complications. But I see it was foolish to expect otherwise."

I asked her what complications she was speaking of, but Muriel would not say. She refused to say anymore on the matter and we finished hanging the laundry in silence.

They are all at the table for supper, though the silence would suggest otherwise. Mr. Hart, Muriel, Jack and young Andy. Even he, in his innocence, is able to sense that he should not disturb the peace, that those gathered here prefer the quiet. That it is in some way necessary. There are no words to be said between the rest. They know everything, all of them.

When Andy is finished eating he asks to be excused and Muriel calls Felicia to take him upstairs to play. I watch the two of them go from the corner where I have hidden myself, wanting to follow them, but knowing that my place is here. These three are the reason I am still here, why I cannot leave Hart's Crossing.

For a time no one speaks or even looks at each other. The only sound is the scraping of the dinnerware upon their plates. The atmosphere is funereal, which stands to reason. A chill runs through me at the thought.

Mr. Hart is the first to speak. "Are you going to tell me what happened?"

"It was an accident Andrew," Muriel says, her voice quivering with emotion.

"A convenient one, no doubt."

Muriel looks away and dabs her eyes with a kerchief.

"It's fine to blame me for it," Jack says. "I deserve it. I blame myself. But it was an accident."

"There are great many things I blame you for," Mr.

Hart said. "But I am not blameless myself. I should have dealt with your treachery long ago."

There is no answer from either Muriel or Jack.

"Nothing to say, is there?" Mr. Hart says. "My only question is about the boy."

Neither of them speak, though they look at each other, a fleeting glance. I am not sure what I see in it. There is an unquenchable fury in me that rises as I look at them and witness that silence. I know the things that they refuse to say. They are looking in my direction as though they have heard something.

Mr. Hart finally grew tired of my obfuscations after several months of them. At no point did I lie to him, but I also failed to tell him much of the truth. He confronted me on the matter when I answered his first question at our latest, and what would prove to be our final, conference with a flippant remark.

Looking down at me sternly, he said, "I don't know why we should continue with these chats if you're going to so willfully defy me. I thought we had an understanding."

I began to deny that I was lying to him, or being willful, but he cut me short, standing up from his chair and exhorting me in a loud voice. "Do not trifle with me girl. You are staying here under my roof, but that can change if I so deem it."

I withered under his gaze and burst into tears, making a pitiful sight of myself. My lack of composure in the face of his wrath left me ashamed at my emotions, which only made me more miserable. Mr. Hart glared at me fiercely, but seemed unable to find any words to say. He looked to me and looked away, as though hoping I would manage to control myself. When I did not he shook his head.

"What is all this about then? What is really going on that you won't tell me?"

"I love Jack," I said, the words bursting from deep within my chest. Once said they could not be unsaid and I shrunk away from Mr. Hart, my eyes focused intently on the floor, fearing what he would say or do.

"You poor little fool," he said, in a voice so quiet that I wondered if he was talking to himself or me. Risking a glance at him, I saw that Mr. Hart was staring off into the distance, his face pale and riven with emotion. It was as though he had aged years in this moment. Without another word he turned and left his study, leaving me there alone to ponder what had just occurred.

I can hear Muriel and Jack talking about me in whispers from her bedroom, where they have gone thinking no one will overhear them. By now they should know that is not the case. The house is empty but for me and Andy, who is napping. I stay by the door and listen as they speak of what has become of me.

"I can still see her face when she realized what was happening. It haunts my dreams," Muriel says, choking back sobs.

"It's no one's fault," Jack says, trying to comfort her. It sounds rote now, for he has said it so many times since my return.

"It is. It is. I brought her here. I was supposed to protect her and instead…" The words are left unfinished.

"It's no one's fault," Jack says again. "It was an accident."

"Our lies brought us here. Yours and mine both."

"They were necessary. Are still necessary. Unless you'd like my father to find out what's been going on. We knew there would be consequences."

"Not like this."

"No," Jack says, sorrowfully. "If I could makes things right for Alice again, I would. But that's not possible."

Muriel doesn't reply and in a moment I can hear her crying. I cannot bear to listen and I go to leave.

"It's no one's fault. Remember, it was an accident…Do you hear something?" Jack says.

"The wind, I think," Muriel says.

It is not.

After my conversations with Muriel and Mr. Hart, where I had revealed my affections for Jack and his for me, everything continued as before. It was as though I had not spoken the words at all. I could not account for it. Though he still claimed to love me, and invited me on his trips to Gleneagle, where we shared our stolen kisses and stolen moments, Jack pretended as though my revelations to his father and Muriel were of no account. He acted as though our love was still a secret that had to be kept, and I played along with him, for I wanted nothing more than to be near him.

Meanwhile, doubt ate away at me. Muriel, too, acted as if all was normal. She did not ask again about my feelings for Jack. It was as if our conversation had never taken place. Only Mr. Hart was truly altered in his attitude toward me. He was as he had been at the beginning of my stay at Hart's Crossing, distant and grim, a looming presence, like a thunderhead upon the horizon.

Two miserable months passed, where I lived a kind of lie, acting the same as Muriel and Jack, as though all was well, even as uncertainty wormed its way into every one of my thoughts. I found myself going over every conversation I had with Jack and Muriel, parsing their words for hidden meanings I had somehow missed, trying desperately to discover the truth, whatever it might be. But I could find nothing and I wondered if somehow Mr. Hart's paranoia had infected me.

Summer turned to fall, the evenings, always cool in the foothills of the Rocky Mountains, became tinged with the promise of frost. I waited and watched and prayed that I was wrong, even as those insidious doubts whispered to me that I was the fool Mr. Hart thought I was.

Toward the end of September Felicia fell ill with a fever that kept her in bed for several days. I took over her chores, feeding the chickens and collecting their eggs, milking the cow, and seeing to the hogs, among other things. On the third day of my chores, as I lingered near the barn door, enjoying a bit of respite after milking the cow, I saw Jack head up the steps and into Hart's Crossing.

The voice of doubt that had crowed at me told me this was what I had been waiting for. What I had dreaded. Mr. Hart was in Calgary, so aside from Andy, Muriel and Jack would be alone. Now I could see for certain what the truth of the matter was, whether those insidious whispers that infected my thoughts were real or imagined.

I crossed the yard and went up onto the porch. Rather than enter the house I circled the veranda, surreptitiously peering through the windows. No doubt I would have looked ridiculous had anyone chanced to see me, but neither Muriel or Jack were visible on the main floor. That should have ended matters there. I should have returned to the barn and milked the cow. Or gone inside to confront them face to face, though the thought of that turned my stomach and left my face warm. But Jack's bedroom was at the corner of the house where the veranda had a pillar I could use to climb atop its roof, from which I could look in through his window.

It was madness to try. I was no climber, especially in my dress, but I was possessed. I needed to know if Jack truly loved me and if I had a future at Hart's Crossing. So I climbed onto the railing and used the pillar to scramble up onto the roof, though not without considerable effort, tearing my dress in the process. I crawled along the roof, which was far steeper than I had imagined, to the window and peered within.

There I saw Jack and Muriel. I don't know whether or not I cried out but they looked up and saw me perched upon the roof. Jack came across the room toward me and, though there was a window between us, I was startled and tried to scramble away. The next thing I knew I was falling, the sky above me and then the ground. The rest I do not remember.

They are at supper again, all of them. Silent as before, the strain evident on their faces. This time I sit with them, in my usual seat, which is empty. I know they will not see me. Sometimes they are aware of my presence, but mostly, I have realized, they pass by oblivious. The reasons for that are best not dwelled upon, though I cannot help it. If I am dead, as I must be, then why I still here, trapped in Hart's Crossing?

They are the reason. It can only be them. They ensnared me in their lies and secrets, used me as a pawn, and now that the consequences of their actions have been made so fatally clear, they cannot release me. They want absolution, but I cannot give it, even if I wanted to. I long to go—whatever awaits me beyond Hart's Crossing calls to me—but I cannot. Muriel and Jack and Mr. Hart hold me here, their silence demanding that I speak.

Let me go, I whisper, but they do not hear.

BORDER CROSSING

1

The moneychangers surround the bus as it comes to a halt next to the concrete platform that leads to the border post, their arms uplifted as though to welcome a returning hero. There are shouts of *dolares* and *pesos* as passengers begin to descend to arrange their exit papers. Some huddle with the moneychangers to negotiate, but most force their way through the crowd and go to the long line that leads into the border post.

George descends with the rest, squinting and looking about, somewhat confused. There are two lines, one snaking into the post, and the other, more formless, leading to some counters lined by glass outside the building. Like ticket booths at a stadium. As he looks at the various signs, trying to ascertain which line he needs, a wiry man sidles up to him.

"You need to go there first, señor," the man says, speaking in accented English. "Get the paper. Then you go inside."

"Gracias," George says, glancing at the man.

"You need a bus?" Here the man points at a bus parked in front of the one George arrived on. "Our bus goes on to Liberia. Still space for you. Twenty neuvo pesos."

"That's all right," George says. "Thank you."

"Your bus ends here," the man says.

"I know," George says, with a nod, already moving to the first line the man gestured to.

On the surface, chaos reigns. The line is disjointed and shifting, with people forcing their way forward and others drifting away before they reach the windows, for no apparent reason. The moneychangers, bus touts, and other sellers ebb and flow around the line, along with others whose purpose George cannot identify. One of these approaches him, a tiny man, who looks as though he can't be older than sixteen, wearing a faded blue uniform and cap.

"Tendría usted que venir conmigo," the man says.

George frowns. It seems unlikely this boy is here in any official capacity. "Necesito mis papeles," he says, in his halting Spanish, gesturing to the windows. The man repeats his demand and George shakes his head, turning away, making clear his intention to remain where he is.

The man is waiting for him after he receives his exit papers and moves toward the second line within the building. "Tendría usted que venir conmigo," he says, sternly.

George frowns in irritation, preparing to dismiss him once and for all. "You better go with him," the bus tout says, materializing from somewhere within the crowd. He nods in the direction of the youth and George looks at him closely for the first time. Though there is no insignia on his cap, or badge on his uniform, he does have a handgun clipped into a holster on his hip. Somehow George did not notice it before. He swears to himself.

"Tendría usted que venir conmigo."

George nods and follows along behind as the youth leads him through another entrance to the border post and into a small, airless room that he surmises is near the center of the building. The youth gestures for him to sit down and leaves him there, closing the door. There is a worn, wooden table at the center of the room, with two chairs on either side. George chooses the side facing the door and sits down. The room is stifling and immediately a sheen of sweat forms on him.

Why has the youth selected him for interrogation? For that is clearly what this is. Is it because he is a gringo?

George has heard there is little corruption along the border, especially with regards to tourists, but that does not mean anything in this particular case. If the youth scents an opportunity, he will act accordingly. Or maybe he just sees something suspicious in George, traveling here alone.

He tells himself to remain calm and closes his eyes, listening to the sounds that reach him. Everything is dim and muffled, so different from the tumult outside. As a test for himself, he summons the route from the room out of the building, as well as any hallways or side routes that might be available. As he works through his conceptualization, he hears the door open.

Two men enter—one, the youth who sequestered him here, and the other an older man with thinning, close-cropped hair and a severe moustache. Both are grim-faced and sit across from him, staring as though he has already been found wanting in some fundamental way. George swallows, wishing he was not sweating quite so profusely, and tries to keep his expression neutral, not giving any indication of the anxiety he feels.

"Passport," the older man says, his accent light.

George reaches into his front shirt pocket and pulls the document out, passing it over. The office studies it carefully, giving each page a great deal of scrutiny, even pulling out a magnifying glass to look at certain parts of it more closely. When he is finished he slides it and the magnifying glass over to his younger counterpart who conducts a similarly thorough survey.

"George O'Bannon. English is fine for you?" George

nods, not replying. "Excellent. You are traveling alone?"

"That's correct," George says. "Why am I here?"

"Routine," the officer says, smiling slightly. "We just have a few questions for you. You are quite well-traveled I see?"

"I enjoy traveling."

"Don't we all. I note that you have been to many of your neighbors in the last two years. And to our fine country. In fact, you've been at the La Miel crossing twice in the last three months. And now you are here in Sapurzo."

"That's true," George says, unwilling to volunteer anymore, though he knows more questions will follow.

"Why?" the officer says in an innocent tone, as though he cannot fathom a reason for George's travels.

"I've been backpacking through Latin America the last two years, as you can tell from my passport."

"I understand. Why so many times, back and forth, across this border? We do not see many tourists here, or at La Miel. Much simpler to cross at Peñas Blancas, if you want to get to the beaches and see the sights. Wouldn't you agree?"

"I like to stay off the beaten path," George says, crossing his arms. He is starting to feel uneasy about this. It is true not many tourists come this way, but that, in itself, is not a reason to suspect him of anything. When, he wonders, will they get to the point?

"I notice you have no luggage with you," the officer says. He glances at his younger counterpart and says something in Spanish that George cannot quite make out. The younger officer answers in the affirmative. "And the bus you are on terminates at Sapurzo."

George stifles a sigh, knowing he has no choice but to endure this. "Plenty of buses on the other side to get me where I'm going."

"And where is that exactly?"

"Is that really your concern? Isn't that their concern?"

George nods in the direction of the border.

The officer smiles thinly. "For now it is my concern. We have to determine whether or not to we will let you cross, or detain for further questioning."

"Shouldn't you be more worried about the people coming in, not the one's leaving?"

"That is for us to determine, wouldn't you say?" The officer replies, allowing a trace of a smile to cross his lips.

"Look, I'm just a backpacker going to meet up with some friends."

"Yet you have no backpack. No luggage at all, in point of fact."

"I left it in San Jose," George says. He pauses, about to explain further, before stopping himself. "Look, I've been across here a couple of times already. You know I'm no threat."

The officer leans back in his chair. "Do we now? That is what we are here to determine."

2

The room seems to grow smaller at the officer's words. He glances at the youth and, without a word, they both stand and walk out, leaving George alone.

What can they possibly suspect him of doing?

He runs his arm across his forehead. It has little effect, his perspiration seeming to bubble up from within at an alarming rate. Obviously he attracted the attention of someone in La Miel when he was crossing back and forth there, though he cannot begin to imagine why. He talked to no one, had no odd encounters, had simply been another traveler passing through.

He puts his head in his hands and sighs, peering down at the table through his fingers. They took his passport when they left, he notices. Is that a sign they want him to pay for its return? Or are they faxing it to La Miel for confirmation he is the man they are looking for?

The answer to both those questions is that he is going to be a good long while in this room.

"Goddamnit," he mutters into his hands. He puts his head on the table, curling his arms around it and closes his eyes, trying to will himself to calm and perhaps to sleep. It has been a long time since he rested—buses never proved themselves conducive for sleep for him—and his exhaustion is fraying the edges of his being, aggravating his anxiety at his current predicament.

Fifteen minutes later, just as he is beginning to drift off, the officers return, sitting across from him. George sits up and looks from one face to the other, but they betray no emotion.

"Where is my passport?" he says, noting their empty hands.

The older officer points at the pocket at his chest. "You will get it back when we are done here."

"When will that be?" George says, trying very hard not to betray his irritation.

"When I am satisfied with your answers."

George gives an exaggerated stretch and leans back in his chair, gesturing with one hand to indicate that they should proceed.

The younger officer glares at him, while the older gives him a small smile. "You think you are clever, do you O'Bannon? You are not so smart as you think. We know exactly who you are."

"Well, you do have my passport."

"Piensa que esto es una broma," the younger officer says. George looks at him and blinks.

"Aren't you going to answer him?" the older officer says, his smile fading from his lips.

"I don't know understand what he said."

"Is that right? Do you know that one of the men who rode with Bolivar was named O'Leary? And one of Mexico's greatest painters was named O'Gorman?"

"What do they have to do with me?"

"It is not as uncommon as one would suspect for someone with an Irish surname to be from these parts."

George shakes his head. "And? You've got my passport right there. I'm Canadian."

"Passports are fluid documents in my experience," the officer says, tapping his finger on the table. "As are nationalities."

"Look," George says, "I can't help you if you won't tell me what this is really about. If you doubt that I'm really Canadian, I suggest you contact the Canadian consulate. You can also notify them that you're holding me and let them know that I have requested a consular representative."

It is the officer's turn to nod, his eyes flashing with anger. "Very well. We will do so. In due time. But for now I want you to answer some questions."

"Gladly."

"Why are you crossing the border here today?"

"I already told you. I'm backpacking and exploring."

"So you say. The same route, every three weeks. You are aware that your government recommends against travel across the La Miel border crossing? And this one as well. These are known crossings for drug traffickers and for various armed groups. Very dangerous."

"They always say that," George says. "If you paid attention to all that stuff you'd never travel anywhere."

The officer glances at his younger counterpart. "Perhaps. You seem to have a healthy disregard for such warnings, though. And you seem to find yourself in such places with a curious regularity. Now, I will ask you again where you intend to travel after you leave Sapurzo."

"San Miguel," George says immediately. "Like I said, I left my backpack there."

"Yes. And where did you travel when you were in our fair nation?"

"San Jose mostly. Rincon for a day."

The younger officer pulls out a notebook and jots something down, causing George to raise an eyebrow. The older officer ignores him. "You were here for four days. When did you go to Rincon?"

"Yesterday. Day trip," George says. He wipes the sweat from his forehead with the palm of his hand, grimacing as he does so.

"Four days without any luggage. You don't find that strange?" the officer says, leaning over to look at what his counterpart had written.

"I had a daypack with me when I came," George says. "I didn't want to bring my bigger pack for a short trip. My hotel in San Miguel is keeping it. Like I said, I was just going to meet some friends for a few days."

"Actually you did not," the officer says in a grave voice. "Before you said you left your bag in San Jose. Now you say in San Miguel. Before you said you were going to meet some friends. Now you say you are coming from meeting with friends."

George has to work hard not to swear in frustration. "I went to meet some friends in San Jose. Now, I'm on my way to meet some friends in San Miguel."

"And your backpack?"

"It's in San Miguel. I just got confused."

"Of course," the officer says, with a sympathetic nod. "And what about your other trips in the last three months? Were they also to San Jose? And Rincon? I note that they too were four days in length. And always on the third week of the month."

"Just a coincidence," George says, knowing how unlikely that sounds, how men like this do not see coincidences. They see patterns. Everything is suspicious to them.

"Indeed."

"Look, it's just a coincidence, like I said. The first time I went because I'd never been before and I wanted to see San Jose. Second time I went back because of a girl. This last time was because some friends of mine were going to be in the country and it was a good place to meet up. And there was the girl, of course."

George is palpably aware of their unwavering stares. The heat is radiating off his face, sweat running into his eyes, forcing him to blink it away. Even as he speaks he can hear how falsely it will ring to their ears. Who went to visit some girl once a month? Why not stay with her?

"Like I said. Coincidence."

The officer pulls out a pen and a notebook. "Write down the girl's name. Her phone number, if you have it. And the hotels you stayed at. I'll check to see if you are telling the truth or not."

George does as requested. "I don't have her phone number. We messaged each other on Facebook."

The officer studies what he has written without replying and then stands and leaves. The youth remains a moment longer, looking out at the where the older officer disappeared, before turning back to George. "You are in trouble," he says in halting English, before rising up to follow his counterpart.

3

The young officer's words frighten George, though he already knows very well that he is in a spot. It is the confiding way the youth spoke that shakes him. They are trying to play him, which means that this is not an idle inquiry, not routine in any way. They were waiting for him.

How did they know? The regularity of his trips these last months tipped them off, and when he crossed over the last time an alert must have gone out to watch for his return. He still does not know what they suspect him of, and he knows the officers will not say. They will wait for him to implicate himself somehow with their questions, like he had with his stupid confusion over San Miguel and San Jose. All these damn towns named after saints.

He contemplates his fate for what seems an endless time, but is in fact only about ten minutes, before the young officer returns to the interrogation room. He is alone, which immediately puts George on guard. Are they trying to play him? Undoubtedly. This is what authorities in every jurisdiction on the planet do.

The youth leans across the table toward George, his expression earnest, which makes him look even younger. "You are in trouble," he says again.

"What do you mean?" George says.

"Salvador," he says, jerking his head in the direction of the door to indicate he is talking about his superior, "is looking for a gringo to solve his problems."

"And I am that gringo?"

The young man nods emphatically. He lowers his voice to a whisper, so that George has to lean forward to hear him. "There are problems lately with the narcos. They have a gringo doing their work for them. He killed some people. We get lots of complaints that we have not done anything. So Salvador thinks we use you to make the complaints stop."

"Why are you telling me this?"

The youth shrugs. "It's not right. I want to help you."

George frowns. It is impossible to know whether this is a ploy, or if this man is genuinely trying to help him. If he is, then this might be his only chance to escape this predicament. If he isn't, then George is ensuring he ends up in an even worse situation.

"How are you going to do that?" George says, glancing around the room.

There is no obvious surveillance—no one sided mirror or camera in the corner of the room—but that did not mean there are no microphones somewhere to pick up what was being said. He has to assume this conversation is not simply between the two of them, that Salvador—or someone—is listening to everything.

"Get you out of here," the officer says.

George tries to read his face, but there is nothing there to reassure him.

"How do you propose to do that?"

"I have your exit papers here. And your passport," the officer pulls out both documents and puts them on the table. The exit paper is signed and stamped and the officer flips the passport book open to show that it has been too. He closes the passport and leans back, leaving both documents there on the table for George to pick up.

He does not, staring at both warily, as though expecting a trap to spring from them. "What do I have to do in exchange for this kindness?"

"Nothing," the officer says. "You must leave now. And you must not return."

George grimaces. It is all so easy. "Not return to Sapurzo? Or not at all?"

"To Sapurzo for certain," the officer says. "Perhaps not at all. He will put your name on a list. It may be others will harass you if you come back, even at other crossings."

"And what about you? Won't you get into trouble if he comes back and I've disappeared?"

"Most likely." The officer gives a vague shrug. "What does it matter? He cannot do anything to me. He knows he is wrong."

That will be unlikely to stop him, George knows, but he doesn't say anything. It makes him even more suspicious. There is no gain for this man to simply release him. He is risking his career for a stranger. Is he really so kind? Is anyone?

The answer, he knows, is no. Still, he reaches across and picks up his passport and exit papers. "Let's go."

4

The officer leads him down the corridor at an unhurried pace, looking calmly straight ahead. George cannot resist craning his head this way and that, as though he might spy someone lying in wait to arrest him. The hallway is empty though, their footsteps echoing down it.

They emerge outside, to find the crowd and the lines unchanged, the moneychangers and touts still shouting. The officer ignores them, leading George away from the buses and the border post south to a road. On either side of the road there is a broad empty expanse where trees have been cleared and then a tall, concrete barrier. Beyond that George can see the tangled trees of a forest.

The road, he knows, leads to the other border post, about five minutes walk away. There he will show his exit papers and passport and have his entry processed and be on his way. Assuming he makes it through this no man's land.

He feels more confident now that they are out of the border post. Partly, it is the fresh air and sunlight. Mostly though, it is the knowledge that he is far safer out here than in that secluded room where no one can see what is happening to him. Although the moneychangers and touts mostly clung to the two border posts, where the buses let off, there are still a few people selling random things to those who choose to walk between the borders. More eyes are better, always.

They have just passed from sight of the first border post when a truck comes roaring down the road, coming to an abrupt stop to block their path. The older officer, Salvador, emerges from the cab, slamming the door shut, his face flush with anger.

"What is the meaning of this Daniel?" he hisses at the younger officer. He is using English, which surprises George. Obviously, he does not want anyone who might chance to overhear them to understand what is being said.

"I am taking him across the border," Daniel says, with a shrug.

"Why?"

"You know he is innocent. He is not a part of this."

"No, you think he is," Salvador says, his face flush with anger. He glares at George. "How many gringos cross the southern border every year? And this man goes through four times in as many months. No, he is up to something. Why do you think he agreed to go with you?"

"He went because I told him to. Because I told him what you were doing," Daniel says.

Both men turn, as if expecting George to say something. He remains silent, staring at them, unsure how this confrontation is going to resolve itself and not wanting to commit to anything until he is certain. The officers turns back to glare at each other, both of them hesitating, clearly unsure of themselves now that they are outside, in front of witnesses. George has to work hard to suppress a grin.

"And what do you think I am doing?" Salvador says at last, keeping his tone neutral.

"You are finding someone to take the fall for the narcos problem. Someone who will not make the narcos angry."

Daniel has his feet planted firmly on the ground, his chest thrust out, his shoulders erect, all to make himself look bigger than he is. The effect is to make him look somewhat ridiculous, at least to George's eyes. The whole situation threatens to become ridiculous now, the two officers interrogating each other, while he and the rest of the world, or at least this little corner of it, look on.

Salvador smiles viciously. "Is that so? I'm the one in the narcos' pocket? Look at this truck. Is that the truck of someone taking narcos dollars?"

Daniel pulls out the revolver at his hip and levels it at Salvador, much to George's surprise and the officer's shock.

"What are you doing?" Salvador says, holding up his hands in shock.

"Are you saying I'm with the narcos?"

George takes a step back and then another, not wanting to be inadvertently shot. He considers continuing on to the next border post, letting these two men settle their dispute, but he worries that might only make the situation worse. The hush of chatter from the touts nearby tells him they have realized what is going on and are watching with rapt attention.

"Don't be an idiot," Salvador says, looking around at the small but growing crowd of onlookers. "You're going to get us both fired."

"Then we're going to let this man go. And you're not going to stop him."

Salvador swallows, not yet willing to give in. "You're either making a stupid mistake, or you're with the narcos."

Daniel flinches, and for a moment George is worried he will pull the trigger. Both he and Salvador exhale at the same moment. "Look," he says, stepping forward to intercede, even as he asks himself what the hell he is doing. "Did you call Angelina? Did you talk to her? She can verify my story."

Salvador grinds his teeth and glares at Daniel, his hands

clenched into fists. "There was no answer."

"Well you've got her number. You can try her again," George says. "I'll be back in about a month's time. Coming through this crossing or at La Miel. If my story doesn't check out you can get me then."

"Is that acceptable to you?" Daniel says. He seems oblivious of the gathering crowd, the stares and the whispers. He does not even look at George, his gaze intent upon Salvador.

"This is a mistake," Salvador says in a pleading voice. "If you let him walk out of here, we'll never see him again. He's gone."

Daniel does not say anything, keeping the gun aimed at Salvador's head. George looks at the older officer, shrugging slightly, as though to say that it is over. Salvador nods in turn, jerking his head for George to go. He does, walking quickly down the road toward the border post, past the onlookers, without a glance back to see what is happening between the two men.

The lines at the next post are as long and as chaotic, but George passes through without incident, emerging from the building onto the soil of a new nation. He makes his way through the crowds of moneychangers and bus touts, past the long queues of buses and taxis, past food stands and stalls selling various trinkets, to what appears to be a side street of the impromptu border town.

He scans the street until he spots what he is looking for, a massive SUV with tinted windows, half-parked and half blocking the street. When the driver sees George, he pulls the vehicle out and meets him on the street. George gets into the passenger side, nodding hello at the driver.

"Hay problemas?" the driver says, not even glancing at George as he turns the SUV around and starts back toward the highway.

"No," George says. "Nada."

ALL DOWN THE LINE

1

The first car, a blue Corsica with peeling paint that was gradually turning it silver, came from the west on Highway Nine. When he reached the turnoff for Hubbard, the driver pulled off the highway and rolled slowly past the ruins of an old gas station and down the main street, such as it was, to the far end of town where a hotel stood at the corner illuminated by one of the hamlet's two streetlights. The other they had just driven past, stationed by the Community Hall, a stolid and square white building behind which sat the town's ball diamonds. There were only a handful other buildings to speak of in the place—even the elevators had been torn down years ago—and only a few of those appeared to be inhabited.

There were no lights on in any of the windows they drove by—hardly surprising, given the hour. Even the hotel was dark, with no vehicles parked in front of it. That too was unremarkable, for it had been years since a room had been rented. Even the strippers passing through to perform made the drive to Loverna for better accommodation. The bar still did a regular business, somehow, mostly the local drunks who couldn't be bothered with an extra half hour of driving to find more pleasant climes.

The Corsica pulled up in front of the hotel, under the streetlight and the driver turned the engine off and the lights as well. Nobody emerged from the car, though there were two people with the driver. They all sat in silence, waiting, looking at the broken and stained stucco that covered the hotel. The driver rolled down his window to let in the cool night air and they listened to the hissing and whirring of various insects.

They didn't have long to wait. The second car arrived five minutes later, coming from the east on one of the gravel roads south of town. The three men in the Corsica could hear its approach, the distinctive grind of car wheels on gravel, long before it arrived and each of them began to shift in their seats in anticipation. The approaching vehicle, a Dodge half-ton, crossed the railroad track and turned onto a road running parallel to it that intersected with main street and the hotel.

The truck engine pulled up alongside the Corsica and cut its engine. Everyone emerged from their vehicles to gather at the steps of the hotel and shake hands.

"Ed. Misty," the Corsica driver said, nodding at both of them. "You know Shane and Burscht."

"Of course," Ed said. "Good to see you Randall. You haven't tried to wake Eduardo up?"

Randall shook his head. "We just got here."

"I'll see if I can get him up," Misty said. He had earned the name when a stripper, of that nom de plum, had managed to take all his casino winnings one drunken evening, along with his clothes, boots and hat.

He strode up the steps to the door and hammered his fist against its heavy steel. When there was no response he repeated the tactic, cocking his head against the door to listen for any sound within. He turned to the others and shook his head.

"For fuck sakes," Randall said, going halfway up the steps and craning his neck above to where a window on the second floor overlooked them. "Wake the fuck up, you lazy fucking half-breed Chinese."

"You trying to rouse the village?" Ed said, something like a grin on his face.

"This fucking guy," Randall said, shaking his head. "Every fucking time. He knows we're coming. He can't stay up or set a goddamn alarm?"

"It is aggravating," Misty said.

"You get that from the dictionary?" Burscht said, bouncing back and forth on his heels.

Misty clenched his fists and came down the steps to where Burscht and Shane stood.

"Hey, hey," Randall said, holding out a hand to forestall him. "None of that now. We're all friends here."

Misty turned to Ed who nodded curtly, but his eyes were leveled at Burscht and they were cold.

Randall turned to Burscht. "Hey, I'm already dealing with one dummy," he said, gesturing up to where Eduardo remained asleep. "Now I gotta worry about you running your mouth? We're trying to conduct a simple business transaction here. Let's not make this more complicated than it fucking is. Alright?"

He looked from face to face and everyone slowly nodded. "Okay then. How do we get this useless fucker up?"

"Maybe try the door first," Shane said, with a shrug.

Everyone watched as Misty clicked down the handle and pulled. The door swung open and they all walked in.

"We could walk away with the whole inventory and he'd never wake up," Ed said, shaking his head in amazement.

"I wish I could say I'm surprised," Randall said. "Go roust the pigfucker and don't be gentle about it."

Burscht went upstairs, while Shane ducked behind the bar to grab them all beers. The rest sat down at the largest table, looking around the room. It was a sight to behold, cluttered with tables and mismatched chairs in various states of disrepair, all thirty years old at least. Off beside the bar, Eduardo had set up a little kitchen on one table, with a hot plate and microwave. Surrounding them on the table were scattered plates and bowls, well-encrusted with food.

"This place smells worse every time I come here," Ed said, lifting his head to scent the air, which was redolent with mildew and ancient carpet, cigarette smoke and urine.

"We're just damn lucky no inspector gives a shit. They'd condemn this place straight out," Shane said, bringing the beers over for everyone.

From above they heard a cry of pain that was quickly silenced, followed by Burscht's angry voice. A few moments later Eduardo emerged, stumbling down the stairs bleary eyed and clutching his nose which was bleeding. Burscht came behind him, a laconic grin on his face, the look of a child who knows he has pleased his father. He led Eduardo to the chair, which Shane pushed out for him, and shoved him down to sit between the two opposing sides, before going to lean against the bar.

"Don't tell me you forgot we were coming again?" Randall said. "Or did your alarm not go off this time?"

"That guy broke my nose," Eduardo said, his voice muffled by his hands.

"Be glad that's the only thing he broke," Randall said, but he gestured to Burscht, who brought a damp cloth over from the bar. Eduardo pressed it to his face to staunch the flow of blood and put his head back so his nose was elevated.

"Now, maybe this is too goddamn complex for your Chinese brain—"

"I'm Filipino, man."

"—but you have one fucking job in this whole enterprise. And that is to be awake when the fucking delivery comes. When you're not, when we have to wake the whole fucking town up just to get a sit down with you, it jeopardizes the whole operation. Not to mention, it makes me look like a shitheel to our friends here."

Randall gestured to Ed and Misty, who sat, staring stonefaced at Eduardo.

"Man, I been asleep like twice when you guys come."

"You've been asleep every time Misty's come by," Ed said. "Don't fucking lie."

Eduardo gave a half shrug of his shoulders and fell silent.

Randall looked at Ed and shook his head apologetically. "Look, Eduardo, like I said, you got one fucking job here. And it's not to keep this bar running. It's to be awake when Misty comes in with the product. Or when we come in with the money. Or when, like tonight, we need to have a meeting to discuss your fucking incompetence."

"Maybe we need to find someone else to take over the bar?" Shane ventured, trying to put something like a threat in his voice.

"Who the fuck else would choose to live here?" Misty said, looking around.

"That is a valid question," Randall said. "But not relevant at the moment."

"I don't know, that picture really brings the place together," Shane said, nodding toward the mural that covered one wall of the bar. It depicted an idyllic scene of a prairie lake of people swimming and picnicking along the shoreline. In front of the mural, which looked as faded as everything else in the place, a stage had been built with a stripper pole at its center.

"You don't have any girls for us either," Burscht said from the bar, drawing a glare from Randall, which froze his smile.

"Girls don't come out anymore. Nobody comes anymore," Eduardo said. "People are wondering why I'm even open."

Randall and Ed looked at each other. "Are people asking you that?" Ed said, an edge to his voice.

"Sure. Guys at the mailboxes joke about it. Even the

assholes that come in here everyday wonder about it."

"Now see," Randall said, leaning forward and grabbing Eduardo's shoulder to pull him close. "This is why we need you awake when we come. Because if people start asking those questions and then they see us showing up at one in the morning, they're going to start thinking we're the answer."

"Right. Sure."

Randall was about to say something more, but he thought better of it and Ed spoke instead, addressing his counterpart. "This is what I am talking about. We've attracted too much attention here, and it's going to bite us in the ass at some point."

"I don't think so," Shane said. "This place has been open for years with nobody coming. Eduardo's not the first moron these people have seen coming in and trying to start something here. They won't be surprised he's here. And they won't be surprised if he decides to go."

"You sure about that," Ed said, and Shane nodded. "Alright, I guess we can live with this arrangement for now. Provided he's awake when fucking deliveries happen."

"Leave that to me," Randall said and turned to Eduardo. "Get the fuck out of here."

Eduardo stumbled from his chair and went back upstairs, still clutching his nose with the cloth. The others watched him go and then listened as the stairs creaked and the floor above them groaned with his weight.

When it was quiet above, Ed leaned across the table. "Now, let's discuss our other problem."

2

Randall gestured with his hand to say that the floor was Ed's.

"Just a minute," Misty said, leveling a finger at Burscht. "He sits down too. He's making me nervous. Looming over everything."

Burscht looked as though he were about to say something in reply, but fell silent as both Randall and Shane glared at him. He pushed away from the bar and sat down in Eduardo's seat.

"We're not going to have a problem here, are we?" Randall said. "We've got a profitable little enterprise going. Let's not let petty squabbles spoil the fruit."

"There's been a lot of money in it," Ed said. "But people here got questions. The law's got questions. And I got questions too."

The room went still after he spoke and they could all hear as one of the refrigerators clicked on and began to hum.

"What kind of questions would those be?"

"Well, there is the issue of the last shipment."

"Bad luck," Randall said.

"So long as your guy doesn't talk," Shane added.

"He won't talk," Misty said.

"Then I don't see a problem here," Randall said, holding out his hands. "No reason why we don't continue like before. Maybe with a few additional precautions."

"See, I don't think it was bad luck," Ed said. "Brad's too smart to get caught like that. He's from around these parts. He knows all the back roads. The ones the RCMP and sheriffs don't sit on. Only way he gets stopped, is because somebody knew he was coming and tipped off the cops."

"And it's gotta be one of my guys did that?" Randall said.

"I know it wasn't any of mine," Ed said.

There was another long silence, with eyes darting from face to face. No one moved, even to take a sip of their beers.

"That's a hell of an accusation," Randall said. Ed held up his hands, open palmed and shrugged.

"Why the hell would we fuck this deal? Why would we fuck ourselves?" Burscht said. "Riddle me that."

Ed did not take his eyes from Randall's. "Are you fucking yourselves? That's what I'm wondering. Cause I hear different things in Saskatoon. I hear that them Quarter boys are looking to move in and set up shop. Best way to do that is to remove the competition."

Randall laughed, though there was no mirth in it. "Christ man. I got enough problems in Medicine Hat. And enough fucking pressure coming from Calgary. I don't need Saskatoon problems to add to it. So forget about that. This is good deal for us. Nice. Simple. And everyone makes out good. Let's not go looking to fuck it up. Alright?"

Ed stared hard at Randall, the other man meeting his eyes without blinking. Finally, as though Randall had passed some sort of unspoken test, Ed nodded in agreement.

"That still leaves one other possibility," Misty said.

Randall nodded. "I trust these two," he said, pointing at Shane and Burscht. "You trust yours, I trust mine. Unless you got evidence saying otherwise, I suggest we leave it."

"What about the Chinaman upstairs?"

"Filipino," Burscht said, with a half-smile. Randall looked at him with a raised eyebrow and he quickly lost himself in his beer label.

Randall shrugged. "There's a short list of people willing to live in this shithole. Quality is not what it used to be, I'm sorry to say."

"He's fucking useless," Shane said. "But he doesn't have the imagination to tip off the cops."

"Maybe," Ed said. "Maybe."

Misty took a long pull of his beer and set it aside. He pointed to the ceiling. "He's hearing all this, you know. You can hear the rats shit in this place, I bet, with the insulation its got."

"No rats in Alberta," Burscht said. "We stop'em at the border."

"Is that so," Misty said.

"Let's not get sidetracked here," Ed said, glaring at the two of them. "Misty has a point though. Your boy can hear everything we're saying here. He knows the drop-off times and the pick-ups. Maybe he's picked up on the routes too."

"You're giving a lot of credit to a fuckhead who can't even wake up when he needs to," Shane said.

Misty started to say something, but Randall held up a hand. He leaned forward, across the table, his voice dropping to a whisper. "Let's allow that your assumption is correct. Eduardo is the weak link. How do we flush that out?"

Everyone considered the question, glancing from time to time at the ceiling, the same thought on their minds. Did Eduardo know they were talking about him, plotting against him?

"We change it up somehow," Shane said. "Or make

him think we are. Make sure he knows. Send one of your guys on a dead run, no product, but tell him that we're doubling the shipment. And then we see if the cops pick him up."

"It makes no sense," Burscht said, cocking his head in thought. "If the cops have flipped Eduardo, they wouldn't want to pick up the shipments. They'd want us during the exchange. Like right now."

Everyone fell silent again, looking at each other from side to side, a nervous energy running through them. No one looked at the door, but they were all expecting a knock. Or a battering ram.

"No product here," Ed said at last.

"Hell of a lot of money though," Burscht said.

There was another awkward silence, which Randall broke. "Money, product, doesn't matter. They still need to flip somebody to bring the enterprise down. And I still say that fucker is too stupid to freelance with the cops. Doesn't mean we shouldn't take precautions though."

"What do you suggest?"

"I don't exactly know Ed. But I like Shane's thought. Maybe you double the number of regular runs, but some of them are dead. Only you know which ones are. We let everyone know. That way it's always a gamble for the cops, or someone's got to tip them off during the exchange. Should be easy to spot whoever is doing that. If the problem is on our end, that is."

Ed thought about it for a moment before nodding. "Alright. We'll do that. Starting next trip. I'll let you know the new schedule."

"Just to be safe, maybe you two shouldn't be involved in any of the meets anymore," Shane said.

"And why would you suggest that?" Ed said, his eyes narrowing.

"Well, the cops'll want to bring in you guys, right. If it's just low-level guys they'll be less likely to roll the operation, I'd guess."

"And if we're not around, there's more opportunity for you to freelance."

"Not at all what I meant," Shane said, holding up his hands.

"Yeah, let's not lose our way here in accusations," Randall said. "But I agree with Ed. If things are going strange, we need to be keeping a closer watch."

"Fine. Let's set something up then," Ed said, one hand picking at the label on his beer. "We also need to revisit the matter of cost."

"How so?" Randall said, not liking that idea at all.

"Well, it's our product and our risk. And if we're doubling shipments, even if half of them are dead, that's more cost to us."

"You know we take the product out of here too," Shane said. "We're taking the same damn risk."

"Have any of your guys been hit? Any of your guys sitting in jail looking at ten years or more?" Misty said.

"You got hit once," Randall said, with a shake of his head. "Once is not a pattern. It happens again, we can talk about a pattern. We can talk about cost. And rats and moles, or whatever the fuck else you want to discuss. But until there's some hard evidence that somebody on our end is fucking us over here, I'm chalking the last shipment up to some bad luck and nothing else."

Ed stopped playing with his beer bottle and pointed at Randall. "I'd love to have your trust. But I don't. And so this is how it's going to be. You want more shipments from us, you're gonna have to pay more. I'm not risking my guys and my product with some half ass reward."

Randall's face went very red as he listened to Ed speak, his hand clenched hard on the table. He opened his mouth to reply, but before he could say anything there was a shout from outside and pounding on the door.

3

All five men whirled to face the door, their jaws going tight. The hammering continued, followed by an incoherent shout.

"Is it the fucking cops?" Burscht said.

"They'd be in here already," Misty said, getting up from his chair.

"Everyone else joined him, looking at each other uneasily. There was a brief pause in the assault on the door, before it continued in earnest again. They could hear whoever it was saying, "I know you're fucking in there," in a very slurred voice.

"Get Eduardo down here to deal with this shit," Randall said to Burscht with a shake of his head.

"Check the back too," Ed said.

Misty and Shane nodded, moving quickly to follow Burscht out the rear of the bar. They headed for the back entrance, while he went up the stairs. Randall stared after them before turning back to Ed. He sighed and sat down in his chair, Ed following his example after a moment. They listened as the drunk outside continued to holler and the floor above them groaned under Burscht's trespasses, neither of them speaking or taking their eyes from the other.

Misty returned first, looking at Ed and shaking his head. "Nothing out there."

"Where's Shane?"

"He's going out front to make sure there's not a world of hurt there."

As Misty spoke Eduardo emerged from the stairs muttering about blood and his broken nose.

"Just do your fucking job and answer the fucking door," Randall said, turning back to Misty. "Why didn't you go with him?"

"If it was a set up somebodied be at the back, right?" Misty said, with a shrug as he sat down. "Unless the whole Hanna detachment's coming through the door here, we got enough firepower to deal with it."

Randall stared hard at Misty, his lips working silently, still hot from Ed's declaration before the drunk had interrupted them. Burscht returned to the table, looking from to face, with a slightly confused expression. As he sat down Eduardo opened the door and beckoned the man outside in.

"Hey Danny, good to see you again."

"Yeah, yeah. I knew you was open see. Knew it when I seen them cars out front. You can't fool me Eddie."

"That's right Danny. Come on and sit down. You want a drink man?"

The four of them watched as Eduardo led Danny, a shuffling man of about fifty years old, hair and whiskers grey, to a seat by the bar. Randall caught Burscht's eye, but he shook his head and shrugged.

Misty leaned forward, speaking under his breath. "Local guy. Nothing to worry about."

"Will he remember us tomorrow?"

"Even if he does, any lawyer would tear his testimony to pieces. Everybody knows he's well on his way to preserving his innards."

"Naw man, I don't need no drink," Danny was saying

to Eduardo. "Just want some smokes from the machine. Ran out. Where these guys from?"

Eduardo looked over at the table where the four men sat and gave a shrug, taking Danny's cash and heading to the cigarette machine. Danny gave a loud sniff and turned to look at the others.

"Where you fellows from?"

"Just on our way to Bassano," Misty said. "Thought we'd stop for a beer, break up the trip."

"Oh yeah," Danny said with a nod, losing interest in them as Eduardo came back with his cigarettes. He took them from the bartender and stood up, muttering something unintelligible and heading to the back where the bathrooms were.

The four men watched him go, no one speaking. Ed shifted in his seat and sighed. Eduardo looked over and raised his hands, to say that he had nothing to do with this interruption.

"Where the hell is Shane?" Randall said, after a moment. Everyone looked at each other, as though someone there must have the answer. None was forthcoming.

Danny shuffled back from the bathroom, stumbling against a chair as he went. "Hey Eddie. Why's there a dead guy in the bathroom, huh?"

Everyone stood in one motion, reaching into jackets, or down to belts, where their guns rested. Eduardo, realizing immediately the disaster that was unfolding, ducked behind the bar. Danny stayed where he was, a confused expression on his face as he looked from where Eduardo had stood only seconds before, to the four men with guns leveled at each other.

"Let's stay calm here," Ed said, looking at Randall.

"That's fucking rich. You don't have someone dead in the fucking bathroom."

"We don't know who killed him."

"Fucking Christ Ed. Open your fucking eyes." Randall

was practically vibrating with anger, his face a deep shade of red. "Misty left at the same time and came back alone. Who the fuck else did it?"

"Your man here came back after Eduardo," Ed said. "He had enough time to do the deed."

"Fuck you," Burscht said, his breath coming in gasps. "Fuck you."

The standoff continued, no one seemingly willing to make the first move, all of them palpably aware that both Danny and Eduardo were watching this unfold. None of them could find their voices, all of them worried about saying the one thing that might spark this tinder keg.

It was Danny who spoke next. "This guy come with you fellows? Hell of a thing."

His words seemed to break the spell cast over the four men. They all turned to study Danny, who nearly stumbled on his feet under their collective gaze.

"Let's handle one thing right now," Randall said and Ed nodded.

He took his gun, which was trained on Randall and pointed it at Danny, pulling the trigger twice in succession. There was not even enough time for surprise to register on his face before Danny slumped to the floor with a sigh.

Randall winced at the sound and lowered his gun, gesturing for Burscht to do the same. "Let's talk this through."

"What about Shane?" Burscht said, his eyes wide in disbelief.

"This is business," Randall said. "Shane knew the risks."

Burscht shook his head, his face colored with emotion, but he lowered his weapon. Misty and Ed both followed suit. Randall sat down and put his gun on the table and the others all did the same.

"Bring us another round," Ed called out to Eduardo.

There was no response from Eduardo. He did not even stir from where he crouched behind the bar.

"Fuck sakes, you want a fucking bullet too," Randall said, slamming his fist on the table. "Bring us another round."

Gingerly Eduardo poked his head above the bar to assure himself that no weapons were pointed in his direction. He brought them each another beer, going slowly around the table to hand them out. His hands were shaking as he did so and he would not look anyone in the eye. When he was done, Eduardo headed toward the back, intending to head back upstairs.

"You stay here," Ed said. "Everybody stays here until we get this sorted out."

Eduardo stiffened at his words, his head bowing in defeat. He went around and sat behind the bar, doing his best not to look over to where Danny lay on the floor, a pool of blood gathering around him.

"It is fucking sorted," Burscht said, as they all turned from watching Eduardo. "This asshole killed Shane and he's gonna fucking pay for it."

"Fuck man," Misty said. "I had nothing to do with it. You and Eduardo had just as much chance to do it as me. And we fucking know he didn't do it."

"What are you saying? What are you saying?" Burscht was shouting, rising out of his seat.

"You fucking know, smart guy."

"Shut the fuck up, both of you," Randall said. "Now it seems to me we've got a lot of fucking problems here. I'm now revising my previous conclusion. I agree with Ed. We've got a fucking rat in the mix somewhere. And it's gotta be one of you two."

"We've got two bodies to deal with too," Ed said. "Do you think anyone heard the shots?"

"You give a fuck about that right now?" Burscht said, still agitated.

"Yeah I do, kid," Ed said. "If somebody heard and called the cops we don't have much time to get things sorted here. No matter what, I intend to walk out that fucking door."

Misty raised his hands. "Depends. Couple of folks live down the street here. Maybe they heard it. Would they call the cops? I don't know."

Randall shook his head. "We can't risk it. We settle this here and now, and get the hell out while we still can. We'll handle Shane's body and you'll handle this dumb cunt. Eduardo will clean everything up."

"What do we do with the bodies?" Ed said, his eyes narrowing.

"I don't care what you do with his. I don't wanna know. Just get it as far away from this place as possible. We don't want any suspicion on this bar or we lose our transit point."

"I think we've already lost it," Ed said.

"Maybe so," Randall said. "We're about to find out. What's your tale?"

He was looking at Misty, who frowned and pursed his lips. "It happened just like I said. We went out back to make sure there wasn't any heat there. There was nothing stirring, so I came back. Shane said he wanted to go around front to make sure the guy was alone."

"Why didn't you go with him?" Ed said.

"I didn't see the use in it. Eddie already had the door open. If there was more than one guy, you were gonna find out pretty quick. Better more of us here to deal with it, I figured."

"That's fucking bullshit," Burscht said, his voice breaking with emotion.

"Let's hear your story junior," Misty said. "You were the last one in the room. You had the best chance to do the deed."

Randall nodded at Burscht, who swallowed. "Alright. I went upstairs and got Eduardo. He had his head on the fucking radiator when I got up there, so I sent him down first and checked out the radiator, see if I could hear what you all were saying too."

"And?"

"Crystal fucking clear, I swear to god. He heard everything man. And I came right fucking down after that. Did not pass go, did not see Shane. And that's the fucking truth."

Ed looked long and hard at Burscht. "Well, if you're both telling it like it was, then there's only one man here who could have done Shane."

As one, they all turned to where Eduardo sat at the bar. But he was no longer there.

4

They all stood, weapons in hand, sending the chairs clattering to the floor in their haste. Randall gestured for Burscht to check behind the bar. Ed covered the front door and Misty the back, while Randall covered Burscht. He went behind the bar, disappearing for a moment, during which everyone's breath went still, before popping up again with a shake of his head.

"Jesus fucking Christ," Randall said, under his breath. "How many fucking ways can this go sideways?"

"We'll check the back and upstairs," Ed said. "You check out front in case he's gone for our vehicles."

Randall nodded and motioned for Burscht to follow him. They went outside to where the truck and Corsica were both parked and were in time to see Eduardo start Danny's truck and throw it into reverse. Burscht fired his pistol wildly and they heard the sound of shattering glass, as Eduardo spun the truck around and peeled out of town, the truck fishtailing wildly spitting up gravel in its wake. Burscht emptied his clip at the disappearing vehicle as Randall shouted at him to stop.

"For fuck sakes man. If the cop's weren't coming before, they are now."

"That little cocksucker deserves to eat lead."

"And he will. He's not getting on a plane back to China tonight."

"Quite the set of guys you got working for you Randall," Ed said. He and Misty were standing at the top of the steps, their guns pointed at the other two men.

"What the fuck is this shit?" Randall said, starting to raise his own gun.

"Drop it," Misty said. "Hands where I can see them. You too kid."

They both did as he said, though Randall was beside himself with fury. "You goddamn motherfuckers. We had a good thing here."

"We did," Ed said, with a nod. "But now it's all gone to shit, all down the line. And I'm just making sure that I get myself paid. Hand over the money."

"I think I'm going to suspend our agreement, until you come to your goddamn senses," Randall said.

"The agreement was null and void, as soon as you let a fucking rat into the operation. Now I'm going to take my buyout, we're going to be on our way, and you can deal with the bodies and cops. Clear?"

Ed took a couple of steps down the stairs, gesturing with the gun for Randall to throw the money at his feet.

"Motherfucker," Randall said, with a vehement shake of his head.

He reached into his jacket pocket and pulled out an envelope thick with bills, an elastic band wrapped around it, and threw it on the ground at Ed's feet. Ed bent down to get the envelope, his gun still raised and his eyes still on both Randall and Burscht. They stayed where they were, looking defeated and angry.

Just before he got his hands on the envelope, another shot echoed through the night. Ed let out a little sigh of surprise as he fell to the ground.

Randall and Burscht stared open mouthed at his fallen body before looking up at Misty. His revolver was aimed at

Randall and he moved smoothly down the stairs to stand over Ed. He looked from face to face, a half-smile pulling at his lips, before crouching down to retrieve the gun and the envelope.

"Motherfucker," Randall said. "Motherfucker. You plan this all along?"

"Don't be stupid," Misty said. He stuffed the envelope in his pocket and stood up with both guns in his hands. "I could've made a mint if you assholes had kept up with this. Fucking Shane spotted the cop car though, so that put an end to that."

There was a pause as both men absorbed what Misty had said.

"You're working for the cops?" Burscht said.

"Sure," Misty said. "Been in the organization with Ed awhile too. Working both sides of the equation, you understand. I was hoping this would be a good retirement fund. Oh well."

"Fucking retirement," Randall said. "How you gonna explain all this to them?"

As he spoke sirens began to sound in the distance, coming from the west. They all turned to peer into the darkness.

Misty turned back to them. "I'll think of something," he said and lifted Ed's revolver up to fire.

STAND BY YOUR MAN

HER PARENTS NAMED her Tammy after the singer of *Stand By Your Man*, a song which she never had much taste for. Country had never been her thing. In high school she acquired another nickname, "trucker fucker", after a rumor started that she waited outside the hotel bar in Loverna for the truckers to come out so she could give them blowjobs. That was not true, or at least not entirely. There had been one guy she gave head to, but she was fairly certain he worked on a seismic rig.

It hadn't mattered though, the name and the story that went with it had stuck and for the rest of high school she was one of those girls. The girl that every guy thought he should try his luck with at a party, whether or not he had a girlfriend. She played the part a few times, mostly out of spite with the boyfriends of girls who taunted her for her sluttiness. It all backfired predictably, with the blame all coming her way.

After high school, lacking the grades and the money to go off to college, she moved into town off her father's farm and took a job at the UFA gas station out on Highway 41. She decided she was done with school and boys and all the drama and nonsense that went with. Now that she was out of school, not interacting with the same one hundred or so horny, judgmental idiots, the nickname and her tawdry reputation began to seem things of the past. She was treated as an adult, accorded that respect, and she began to get it into her head that she deserved a man not a boy, though she did not quite know what that meant.

It led her into the arms of Gary Seedstrom, the UFA store manager, a married man with two young kids. He told her he would leave his wife, that he loved her, but he was no different than the high school boys who leered at her and looked her up and down, asked for a blow job and called her a slut when she didn't comply. Worse, he was a crook and a murderer and tried to use her as an alibi to cover up all his schemes.

That all ended in disaster when Gary was killed himself. Before that, Tammy had the satisfaction of exposing his lies to his wife. That had proved a fleeting and ultimately hollow victory, for soon after the whole town knew about her and Gary.

The fact she was discovered, bound and naked in Russell Pedersson's bed, the night Gary's killer was caught also became general knowledge. Never mind that Russell had been tortured and she had been threatened, the whole thing was so sordid no one in town could stop talking about it. Walking the streets of Loverna felt like high school all over again.

Tammy left after that, unable to face everyone's stares, the way they seemed to be accusing her of some crime, as though her continued presence implicated her in some way. She was tired of the way conversation would lull when she approached, and of the whispers that were forever behind her. *I know you're talking about me*, she longed to turn around and say, but she never did. The hurt in her mother's eyes had been the worst of all, worse even than her father calling her damned fool.

She went to Medicine Hat, intimidated by the idea of

going to a big city like Calgary or Edmonton, and not knowing where else to go. It was a place she had visited often while growing up, so it offered the comfort of familiarity, with enough of the unknown to still be enticing. Most of all she got something like the anonymity that she craved, with no one that she passed on the street knowing or caring who she was.

Her first job was at a bar named Checkers, where she worked as a waitress. The tips were good, especially after she followed one of the other girl's recommendations and bought herself a couple of short skirts that accentuated her legs. It was more than enough to live on.

She made a mistake her second week, sleeping with one of the bar managers in his office at the back. Somehow everyone knew within the space of a day and, unbeknownst to her, the manager had also been sleeping with one of the other waitresses. The other girls all turned against Tammy, giving her looks that she was only too familiar with.

After that she kept to herself on the job, minding her business and being careful not to go home with any of the staff, or even the customers. That did not stop them from trying, but she soon became adept at slipping out of grasps and removing hands from where they were not wanted, all while keeping her smile firmly in place. She learned how to keep her guard up around people, gradually adjusting to the disorientation of being in a place where everyone didn't know each other and where you didn't have conversations with people while going to get the mail or buy groceries.

It was all very strange and she was left feeling lonely. In spite of everything, she found herself missing Loverna. That all changed when she met Kevin Burscht. He was not like the men she had met before. He was different.

Kevin worked in the oilfields, though he was vague on the specifics of what he did. Something about well site reclamation and parts. He didn't talk much about it, which suited Tammy fine. They met at a Tim Horton's, where Tammy had gone for breakfast late one morning after working till close at Checkers. The line up was long and the service terrible and she fell to talking with the genial young man with a smile that made her go weak in the knees.

He invited her to join him for breakfast and they talked for over an hour, long after they both finished their coffee and bagels. Kevin asked for her number and they arranged to meet for a drink later that week. It all felt so different from the happenstance and calamity of her other relationships, which she now realized had not been real relationships all. This one was.

Kevin traveled a lot for his work, which meant Tammy saw him only a day or two a week, but that was fine by her. She was learning to enjoy the time she spent on her own, after so many years living underfoot at home and in Loverna. It was surprising to realize how suffocating that had been and how freeing this felt. Her, as yet, ill-defined relationship with Kevin felt of a piece with this new life she was constructing.

Jennifer, the one girl at work who still talked with her, told Tammy to watch herself. "Who knows what he's getting up to when he's out there traveling. You can't trust him."

Tammy knew as well as Jennifer what men like Kevin got up to in the small towns they traveled to for work, but she didn't worry about him. She trusted him, for reasons she couldn't put into words. He was different. Maybe it was his attentiveness, the way he listened to what she said and considered it. Most of the men she had known had seemed only to be waiting for her to finish whatever she was saying so they could start taking her shirt off. He wasn't like that.

When they were together, during dinner or after sex, Tammy would go on and on about her future and her dreams, things that she had never shared with anyone. Kevin would listen and encourage her, but he shared little of his own thoughts. Tammy was so caught up in the emotion of actually being able to say these things to someone that she didn't notice. And when she did, she pushed that thought aside, telling herself it was because he was a guy. Men don't like revealing themselves, she told herself.

One night, when he had come over very late, after the initial urgency of passion had left them and they were lying in each other's arms, Tammy mentioned that she wanted to move to Vancouver.

"Why?" Kevin said, his voice dim, as if he were already starting to drift off to sleep.

"I don't know. I've never seen the ocean before. I'd love to see it. And it just seems so cool. There's so much happening there."

"Mmm," Kevin said.

Tammy looked over and could see his eyes were half-closed. "What about you? Where do you want to live?"

"Not Vancouver."

"Why not?"

"I'm from there," Kevin said, a pained frown crossing his face and then vanishing.

"Really," Tammy said. "And you wouldn't go back?"

There was a long pause, during which she wondered if he was asleep, before Kevin replied. "I can't."

"Why not?" Tammy asked, but received no reply as Kevin's breathing deepened and slowed.

"What do you think he means?" Tammy asked Jennifer when they were next on shift together.

"Nothing good."

Jennifer was only a year or two older than Tammy, and with her sleight frame she looked even younger, but she seemed to have decades more experience, at least to the girl from Loverna. She had, it seemed, dated every kind of bad man—and every man was bad in some kind of way, according to her. That was a fact as inescapable as gravity.

Everything about Kevin was a mark of suspicion for her. His absences for work, his refusal to share much about his feelings or his life. All of it was proof that he was no good.

"You only can't go back to a place if you've done something wrong. Vancouver's a big place. If he's worried about being found there, it must be something really wrong."

Jennifer had a way of speaking that gave her an authority. She sounded like she knew what she was talking about. And yet Tammy wasn't sure.

Nothing more came of the conversation, no matter how Tammy tried to pry and steer Kevin in that direction. He seemed oblivious to her attempts and wouldn't say anything more on the matter. Not when she brought up his parents, or high school, or his friends. It was as if that part of him had ceased to exist once he left British Columbia.

Tammy told herself not to let it bother her. There could be a lot of reasons for that, after all. Not everyone had happy childhoods they wished to return to, as she well knew.

She did not dwell on the matter. For all his reticence and his frequent absences, he was the most present of the men she had been with. After three months she contemplated telling him she loved him, but her courage failed her. It seemed perilous to risk upsetting something that was so precious to her and seemed so perfect. For she knew nothing this good could last forever.

Everything changed the night Tammy came home from Checkers to find Kevin already in her apartment.

She had a small one-bedroom in the basement of a dumpy three-story apartment building, just across the railroad tracks from downtown. The building was white with brown trim, and in desperate need of a coat of paint, as was her apartment, which had been indifferently cleaned before she took it over. Tammy was mostly oblivious to these faults. It was a place all her own, proof, however humble, of her success at living away from her parents.

She was so startled when she came through the door to see him fiddling with the fan above the stove that she let out a little scream.

"Babe, don't worry. It's just me," Kevin said, rushing over to take her into his arms and close the door to the apartment.

"What are you doing here?" Tammy said, pulling away from his kiss.

"Sorry," he said. "I meant to text you, but I thought I would surprise you."

"By breaking into my house?"

"Yeah. It seems really stupid now. I'm sorry. I should of texted." Kevin smiled and shook his head.

How often, Tammy wondered, had she let things go because of that smile? She felt something twist in her stomach.

"What were you doing with the fan?"

"Oh," he said, glancing over at it. "Nothing. I was just trying to fix it. Didn't you say it was broken?"

"It is," Tammy said, walking over to look at it. She threw her purse on the table and looked back at Kevin. "It's one in the morning. Why were you trying to fix it?"

Kevin shrugged and tried his smile again. "Bored I guess. I didn't think you'd be around for a bit."

"I got let off early. Place was dead." Tammy walked into the living room, flicking on the light to look around. What else had he been doing while he was here? Everything was in the mess she left it. She wasn't sure how to feel, afraid or angry, and her tiredness was confusing her thoughts.

"Look, I'm sorry babe. I thought it would be funny. But it wasn't." Kevin said, coming up to put an arm around her.

"No, it wasn't," Tammy said, shrugging out from under his arm. "Don't do that again. How'd you get in here anyway?"

Kevin shrugged. "I convinced the building manager to let me in."

Tammy stared hard at him. He had to be lying, she thought. Roberta would never let him in. Had she even seen him before? The longer she thought about it, the more uneasy she became. All the questions she had pushed aside over the last months came to fore. Who was this person standing across from her?

"I'm going to bed," she said at last. "I'm tired. We can talk about this in the morning."

"Sure babe," Kevin said in a meek voice, following her into the bedroom.

He didn't try anything when they got into bed, which reassured her somewhat, but it was still a long time before she managed to drift to sleep. She could not shake the feeling that she was lying next to a stranger about whom she knew nothing.

The next morning when she woke up he was gone.

Kevin's disappearance shook Tammy even more than his breaking into her apartment had. The latter could be explained away as an exceedingly stupid prank gone wrong, if she chose to believe him. He had clearly meant no harm in it and had obviously felt guilty. But leaving without a word of goodbye cast all that had happened before in a new light, especially his guilt. She found herself going over every odd thing he had ever done or said, every explanation he had given for his absences or appearances. There were more questions than answers to be found there.

He left a note, which he had scrawled on the back of an opened envelope, that simple read, "Call you later."

When Tammy read it she burst into tears, crumpling it

up and throwing it across the room. The rest of the day passed in haze, colored by the darkness that seemed to be closing around her thoughts. Her relationship with Kevin seemed to be at an end. How could she continue if she couldn't trust him?

She asked the question and tried to find an answer that would allow them to stay together, but it was no good. Worst of all, she didn't even know if he wanted to stay with her. She had no idea what he wanted at all.

She checked her phone at least every ten minutes for a text from Kevin, but none arrived. Every hour she talked herself out of sending him a message. When she went to work that night she was in a fog, forgetting orders and taking drinks to the wrong tables.

"What the hell's the matter with you?" Jennifer asked her, when they had a moment together in the kitchen waiting for their food orders, and she burst into tears.

"Oh Jesus," Jennifer said, with a shake of her head. "Forget him. I told you. He's not worth another minute of your time."

"You're right," Tammy said, but she could not just forget Kevin. His smile was there every time she closed her eyes and, for the rest of her shift, she found herself catching a glimpse of what she thought was him out of the corner of her eye, only to turn and see a stranger.

It was nearly four in the morning when she returned home from work. Closing had been late, with no one seemingly willing to leave after last call and every task taking an inordinate amount of time and effort. She was exhausted and numb by the time she came to her apartment door, thoughts of Kevin fading for the moment. She wanted nothing more than to lie down and sleep.

The first sign that something was wrong was that her door was already unlocked. She noticed it absently as the bolt did not turn along with the key. The weight of that fact had not settled upon her by the time she stepped through the door and went to turn on the light, only to realize it was already on. And that she was face to face with a handgun.

Tammy screamed, or started to, before the man holding the gun swung it hard against the side of her head, sending her crashing into the wall.

"Quiet bitch," the man said, shutting the door to her apartment after a quick glance up and down the hallway.

Tammy looked up at him, stunned and fearful, a slight buzzing echoing in her ears. He glared at her, his lips curling into a snarl. He might have said something else, but Tammy didn't hear.

"Are we trying to wake up the whole neighborhood, *Brian*?"

That question, pointed and angry, she did hear. The voice, deep and gravelly—not unlike her father's, which was an odd thought—came from the living room. A man, broad shouldered and with a thick belly ducked around the corner. The fat of the belly did not seem to extend beyond his stomach to the rest of his frame, not unlike many of the older men from Loverna. Beyond the gut, he looked very much like a rancher, with wrangler jeans, cowboy boots and a snap button shirt. He looked at Tammy, and then at the man with the gun, with a critical eye.

"She started to scream, boss," the other man said, by way of explanation. He was young, no older than Tammy, by the look of him. His hair, which it looked like he had spent hours preparing, was shaved along the sides and long on top, precisely combed over, with not a strand out of place.

"Of course she did. You were pointing a gun at her."

"You told me to have it ready," Brian said.

"Ready doesn't mean pointing it at someone. It means being able to. Now she may have woken up the whole damn building."

"I didn't mean to," Brian said. His voice had a tone that made him sound perpetually offended.

Tammy risked putting a hand to her cheek, which throbbed from the impact of the gun. All she could think was that she wouldn't be able to go to work tomorrow. Not with a bruise on her face. Maybe Jennifer knew how to cover bruises with makeup.

"Come on, girl," the older man said, motioning to her with his hand. "We'll know soon enough if the cops are on their way. What's your name?"

"Tammy," she said, climbing unsteadily to her feet. She had to lean against the wall to support herself, her whole body shaking.

"Come on, girl. Sit down," the man said, pointing at the couch.

Tammy went over and sat on its edge. She could not stop thinking about Lyle Hargreaves and his gun and how he had tied her up and she had listened to him torture Russell Pedersson. This after he had killed Gary Seedstrom and beaten his wife. Was it just her fate to run into maniacs with weapons?

The older man came and sat at the other end of the couch, attempting a calming smile. Brian, the gun now hidden in the back on his pants, lurked near the entryway, just within Tammy's sightline, pacing about as though he wasn't sure where he should stand.

"Quit moving around Brian," the man on the couch said. "You're making me nervous."

Brian looked as though he wanted to argue the point, but he stopped moving and leaned against the corner of the entryway to the living room, glaring at both Tammy and the older man.

"You can call me Arnold," the older man said, turning his attention back to Tammy. "It's a pleasure to meet you Tammy. I'm sorry for circumstances. It couldn't be helped."

"What do you want?" Tammy said.

"That's fair, that's fair," Arnold said, nodding vigorously. "Fair to be mad. But don't blame me. It's really your boyfriend's fault, all of this."

"Kevin?" Tammy said, incredulous. Her stomach lurched at the thought of him. Were these men responsible for his strange appearance and disappearance the night before?

"He is your boyfriend, no? We know he is, I should say. We know a great deal about Kevin, because I make it my business to know everything about the people who work for me."

"You work in the oilfield?"

"Ha. No," Arnold seemed very amused. "Is that what he told you? No, no we do not. What we do isn't important. What is important is that Kevin has taken something of mine. A great deal of it. And I want it back."

Tammy blinked. All the blood seemed to be rushing to her head at once. It was not a surprise that Kevin had lied to her, after all that had happened the night before, but it still hurt. She had hoped that somehow he would prove innocent of her worst suspicions. But the presence of these two men told her that her worst suspicions did not even scratch the surface of what Kevin had done.

"I don't know where he is."

"I do," Arnold said. "That's why I'm here. To get back what he stole from me."

"I don't know anything about that."

Arnold frowned. "That's disappointing to hear. I had really hoped this would be easy. If you insist on making it complicated it will be."

"I really don't know what you're talking about," Tammy said, choking back a sob of fear.

"Very well," Arnold said, shaking his head in disappointment. He turned to Brian and nodded.

"Don't think about screaming. It will only make things worse," Arnold said in a stern voice.

It was as though he had been reading her mind. Tammy had been contemplating yelling for help as she watched Brian comprehensively destroy her meager possessions, in a search that she knew would turn up nothing. The cupboards in her kitchen had been emptied, the drawers dumped on the floor, and everything in refrigerator had been studied to see if somehow hid whatever it was Arnold thought Kevin had given her.

"He didn't give me anything," Tammy said again as Brian tore apart the cushions on the couch, having done the same to her one chair. "He didn't even tell me who he was working for."

"All the more reason to leave it here," Arnold said, not even glancing in her direction. "He thought it would be safe here."

"It's probably at his place."

"You don't think we already looked there?" Brian said, the annoyance in his voice real this time.

"Shut up and keep looking," Arnold said, glaring at his counterpart. Turning to Tammy he said, "You'd best tell us what you know. I don't want to do this, but I will do what I have to. And it will be very unpleasant for you."

"I can't tell you what I don't know."

Tammy glared at both men, her anger quelling her fear. She cursed herself for ever trusting Kevin. Jennifer was right, you couldn't trust any man. All of them lied. Everything about Kevin had been lies, all of which she had been stupid enough to believe. She remembered that smile, how it had made her swoon, and how he had used it to deflect her attention whenever she asked questions he didn't want answers to.

His lies had obviously extended to these criminals as well, but it seemed she was the one who would pay the price for that. Life was just so damn unfair.

Tammy glanced at the clock on the microwave, which was within the line of sight from where she sat and saw that it was almost five. People would be starting to wake up soon. If she ignored Arnold's threats and made a scene, someone would likely call the police. But help would probably not arrive in time to save her.

The question was: how far Arnold was willing to go to get back what he felt was owed him?

If he was to be believed, it was very far indeed. Just as important, Tammy realized, was how angry he would be once he discovered that whatever Kevin had stolen wasn't in her apartment. Would he blame her? It was a bad situation and only likely to get worse. Reluctantly, Tammy decided to wait. There seemed no other choice.

Arnold grew quieter and quieter, his anger growing more and more evident on his face, as Brian continued to find no trace of what they were looking for amidst Tammy's things. He no longer threatened her, he just stared at her, grinding his teeth together, insinuating her fate with his eyes.

Brian finished with the kitchen and living room, shaking his head at Arnold, and went to the bedroom. The older man motioned for Tammy to follow him and she sat on the far side of her bed, watching as Brian emptied her closet and her drawers. Arnold sat on the other side of the bed, his eyes darting from Brian to her, his glare becoming more and more pronounced.

Tammy felt lightheaded, and she still ached from the blow she had taken from Brian, but she refused to break as Arnold seemed to want her to. She was not going to give them the satisfaction. Not yet, anyway.

"There's nothing here," Brian said at last, kicking at the panties and socks he had dumped on the floor. He turned to look at Arnold, who shook his head.

"Last chance, girl," he said. "Are you going to keep standing by your man? All he did was lie to you. Now, tell me where my fucking money is."

Tammy flinched. "He didn't give me any money. He didn't tell me about any of this. I don't know."

Arnold grew very still, his anger seeming to move inward. "You goddamn stupid bitch. This is how it's going to be, is it? Don't say I didn't warn you."

Brian grinned insolently at Tammy, who could feel the blood go from her face. She backed away from the two men into the corner of the bedroom, her whole body starting to shake again. The apartment building seemed absolutely still, as though it too was holding its breath.

Arnold looked at Brian and seemed on the verge of telling him to do something when his phone rang, the annoying pulse of the ringtone cutting through the quiet like an alarm sounding. Tammy jumped at the sound, emitting an odd gasp that made Brian chuckle and leer at her. Arnold glared at the younger man as he fished out the phone and looked at the display. He held up a finger, warning everyone to stay quiet, as he took the call.

"Yes. What is it?" Arnold stepped out of the bedroom and into the short hallway that led to rest of the apartment, his back to the other two. Brian raised an eyebrow at Tammy, motioning behind his back to where his gun was tucked away, and smiled. She closed her eyes and resisted a shudder.

"Goddamnit. Are you fucking kidding me? Jesus….Alright. Give me ten minutes and I'll be there."

The call ended and Arnold returned to the bedroom. Something had happened, it was obvious from his grim expression. "I have to go," he announced.

"Now?" Brian said.

"What did I just fucking say," Arnold said. "You stay with her. Don't let her out of your sight. I don't need this situation to go more sideways than it already fucking has."

He left without another word, leaving Brian and Tammy standing in the bedroom staring at the empty space where he had stood.

Brian appeared as surprised and uncertain as Tammy felt. Whether that was good or not, she did not know. She started out of the bedroom, only to have Brian snap out of his confusion and move to block her way.

"Where do you think you're going?" he said, moving

his hand behind his back to where his gun was.

"I'm going to sit down. Who knows how long he'll be."

"You can sit down here," Brian said, gesturing to the bed. "And don't worry about how long it'll be. That's not your concern."

Tammy wanted to tell him that it very much was her concern, given she was the one being held prisoner, but she decided not to push him. Who knew how he would react without Arnold to keep him in check? She sat on the edge of the bed, looking down at the mess on the floor.

"You know, I could be out of your hair if you just gave us what we need," Brian said.

"I already told you, I don't know what you're talking about. Kevin didn't tell me anything."

Tammy did not even bother to glance over at him as she spoke. Brian moved over from the door to stand in front of her, staring down at her until she looked up. He grinned.

"I bet. You know, if you're not going to tell me where the money is, we can do something else to pass the time. Kevin told me how good a piece of ass you were."

Tammy fixed him with a poisonous glare. "Could you handle mussing up your hair?"

Brian flinched, his grin fading. "Think you're funny? Well, the jokes on fucking you. You think you were Kevin's only girl? No way, bitch. He had a pussy in every port. You think he was off working in the oil field. No, he was running drugs to shithole towns like the one you're from. And he had a girl there like you in every one of them. He told me."

Tammy worked hard not to look as devastated as she felt. "You're just jealous he could get a girl. The closest you could get is jacking off to his stories."

Brian shook his head, his lips curling into a vicious sneer. He reached back and pulled the gun from his pants and aimed at her. "You think you're funny, do you bitch. Real cute. I know one girl I could get right now."

Tammy went still. *This is not happening*, a part of her mind said.

"Oh, nothing to say now?" Brian said, triumphant. He took a step closer to her, his legs nearly touching her own. "Come on, let's see what those lips can do besides talk."

"Please," Tammy managed to say.

"Begging for it, are you? I tell you what. Take off your top and I'll see."

Tammy shook her head. "Please," she said again.

They were interrupted by a loud knock on the door.

"Tammy Fairchild."

The words were spoken in a loud authoritative voice with the air of a command, though none had been issued. They hung there for what felt like minutes, until a second knock sounded on the door.

"Fuck me," Brian whispered under his breath.

He turned away from Tammy and tucked the gun back into his pants and started toward the door. As soon as he was out of the bedroom, Tammy leapt to her feet and slammed the door shut, locking it with a twist of the handle.

"Hey," Brian said, in surprise from the other side.

"Help me. He's got a gun," Tammy screamed as loud as she could, diving under the bed.

A tumult of sound followed. Brian called her a "fucking bitch," as the police knocked down the front door. There was crashing and further yells and orders, all seeming to come at the same time. Tammy closed her eyes and forced herself to breathe until it was quiet.

"Tammy Fairchild?" This was followed by a gentle knock at the door. "It's Constable Malbeck with RCMP. We've detained the suspect. It's safe for you to come out."

Tammy waited a moment to gather herself. She would not face the police a sobbing mess again. When she opened the door she was greeted by a familiar face. It was only then that she connected the name with the tall and gangly, young constable with the crewcut hair. He had been there that night when Lyle Hargreaves was caught. She felt her face go red.

"Tammy Fairchild. I knew that name was familiar," he said, nodding in recognition. "We have to stop meeting like this."

She attempted a smile. "I guess."

Another officer, a striking woman with black hair and flashing dark eyes entered the apartment. "Constable Breton, this is Tammy Fairchild," Malbeck said, gesturing between both of them.

"You okay?" Breton said, frowning.

"Yeah," Tammy said. "I think so."

"Maybe you should sit down. We have some questions for you."

"Okay." Tammy went over to the couch, picking her way among the debris that Brian and Arnold had left behind. She and Breton picked up the remnants of the cushions and set them back on the couch.

"You want some water? Coffee maybe?" Malbeck called from the kitchen, as Constable Breton sat down beside her.

"Maybe some coffee," Tammy said, in a small voice.

"Did you know the man who was here?" Breton said, as Malbeck busied himself digging through the mess in the kitchen.

"No," Tammy said. "There was two of them."

"Okay. Did they mention their names?"

"Brian was the one you arrested. Arnold was the other guy. He was in charge."

Constable Breton nodded, pulling out a notebook and a pen. "And when did this Arnold leave?"

"Maybe half an hour ago. At the most. He got a phone call. It sounded like something had gone wrong. He said he had something to deal with and made Brian stay to watch me."

Breton and Malbeck exchanged a glance. "I think we

know what that phone call was about," she said. "Why were they here in the first place?"

Tammy winced at the suspicion in the constable's voice. "They were looking for something. They thought my boyfriend had hidden it here."

"What was that? Do you know?" Malbeck said, handing her a cup of coffee. "Do you take anything in it?"

Tammy shook her head. "Thanks, no. Money, I guess. I don't know."

"Your boyfriend is Kevin Burscht?" Breton said.

"Yeah. How'd you know?"

"We found your number on his cell phone," Malbeck said. He paused. "I'm afraid we have some bad news. He was murdered last night at the bar in Hubbard, with a few other men. They were all in the drug business. So was Kevin, I'm afraid."

Tammy nodded. She braced herself for a flood of emotion, but none came. The last two days had been so full of lies revealed that she no longer knew what to feel about Kevin. And she was so tired. Even now she could feel her exhaustion, a wall behind her eyes advancing ever nearer.

"You don't look surprised?" Breton said.

Tammy shook her head. "I don't know. Everything I thought I knew about him was a lie, I guess. If he's got friends like Brian and Arnold, then I guess it's not strange that he got himself mixed up into whatever this was."

"Right," Breton said. She frowned and looked as though she wanted to press Tammy on the subject, but Malbeck interjected first.

"When did you last see Kevin?"

"Last night," Tammy said, thinking back to their final strange encounter. She still did not understand why he had come by and then left without so much as a goodbye. Obviously things had been happening and events had moved beyond his control. But why come here and drag her into this mess?

"What was he doing here?" Malbeck said.

"Nothing. He just came by to surprise me. And then he left before I got up this morning. Didn't even say goodbye."

Tammy choked back a sob that emerged from somewhere so deep within herself she was not even aware of it. She was so tired. All she wanted was for these officers to leave so she could lie down and sleep on the couch. She had work tonight, the thought occurred to her. All this and she had to go to work.

Breton seemed annoyed with her. Her frown deepened and she said, "Anything else you should be telling us?"

Tammy shook her head.

"First you get mixed in that murder, and with a boss who was a criminal, if I recall the details. And now you're hanging around with a known drug dealer. A drug dealer who was killed near where you grew up. You're going to tell me that's a coincidence."

"He told me he worked in the oilfield," Tammy said. "I didn't know."

"You didn't know. Guy's never around, working odd hours, and you don't get suspicious?" Breton shook her head. "I don't understand girls like you. Always standing by your man. Someday you're gonna grow up and realize how stupid you're being protecting someone like him. You're only hurting yourself."

Tammy looked up from the floor and into the constable's eyes. "Do you have any more questions. I'd like to get some sleep. I have to work tonight."

Malbeck was staring at his partner, his expression pained. "No, no," he said quickly. "We'll be in touch, of course. Probably have some questions about the two gentlemen who were here earlier. But we can give you a chance to recover before we go any farther."

He stood up and Breton followed his lead a moment later. Tammy followed them to the door and locked it behind them, though it seemed like a useless precaution now. She stumbled back to the living room looking down at the ruins of her life, wondering why she had ever trusted Kevin and why he had brought all this upon her. Had he even cared about her at all?

She pushed those thoughts aside and lay down on the couch, closing her eyes and trying to sleep. But sleep would not come, her mind was still whirring with visions of the last day. Brian hitting her with the gun and tearing the place apart. Arnold, gruff and sinister, looking her over like she didn't even exist. Breton's judgmental glare, the way she thought she knew exactly what Tammy was.

And Kevin in the kitchen, coming to the door to kiss her. To hide what he was doing, she realized. She had been early and he hadn't been expecting her. There was no surprise. He was planning to be gone before she returned.

Her eyes flashed open and she got up and went into the kitchen. Brian had emptied all the cupboards and drawers, and her meager supply of dishes and pots and glasses lay scattered on the counter. She opened the cupboards to check them, but they were all bare. If Kevin had actually left something here, surely Brian would have found it. He had been very thorough.

What was it Kevin had said when she asked what he was doing in the kitchen? She tried to remember through the fog of her exhaustion.

The fan. Above the stove.

He had said he was fixing it. It hadn't worked since she had moved in. Tammy went to it now, looking it over and reaching up underneath. There was nothing there, not that she could see or feel. She pulled at it and it came away from the wall, opening a space that she could slip her hand up. There her fingers encountered an envelope.

She opened it first and saw it was full of twenties and fifties and hundreds. There had to be thousands of dollars there. It was only as she was setting the envelope down, trying to collect her thoughts, that she saw the writing on the back of the envelope. It said "Vancouver" and underneath Kevin had drawn a smiley face.

Tammy picked it up, her hands shaking, and began to cry.

DRIFTING

1

The Bull-a-Rama was over; the stock already loaded into trailers and on their way back to the Hertel Brothers Ranch, while the tented area behind the stands was in the process of being cleared out for the dance. Dane finished the beer he was drinking, crushing the can underneath his boot heel and throwing it away, while waving at the other cowboys who were gathered behind the corrals drinking and waiting for the dance to start. He headed off across the rodeo grounds, around the stands and towards the RV Park filled with trucks and campers.

"Hey babe," he said when he found her trailer, tucked in with several others around a small stand of trees. She squinted at him without responding as he plopped himself down on the picnic table beside the trailer.

"You reek," she said, "How many you had so far?"

"Emma," he said.

"You gotta drive to Maple Creek tonight."

He shook his head and took out his can of Copenhagen. "Nah," he said, "We're going first thing tomorrow. Colton thinks he's got a line on some girl."

Emma rolled her eyes. "You both better not get too out of hand then. You're gonna have to get up pretty early to make it for the draw."

"Only five thirty," he said. "Besides, don't you want to spend a night with your man?"

She squinted at him again, but sat on the knee he offered and put her arms around his neck.

"Only if you behave," she said, kissing him quickly and then standing up to go into the trailer.

"When have I ever not?"

"Every time," she called from inside the trailer and he smiled and went off to find Colton.

The dance started a little after nine, the deejay putting on a steady rotation of country music with brief digressions into AC/DC and Led Zeppelin among others. The tent, which roughly formed the dance floor, was open at all sides so that people could come and go. It had been set up in the event of rain, but there was not a cloud in the sky as the sun began its descent, ribbons of red and gold streaking the western horizon. The bar was at the opposite end of the tent from the deejay's setup and in the first hour of the dance it was surrounded by a milling crowd while the rest of dance floor area was more or less empty. As drinks were finished the center of gravity of the place began to shift away from the bar, with couples pairing off and heading out to two-step. Even those not dancing turned their attention to those who were, nodding their heads to the rhythm as they sipped their drinks.

Dane lost track of Emma when he ducked out of the dance to smoke a joint with a few of the other cowboys. This was after he had nearly started something with Gord Steckley, another guy on the circuit who had been talking with her at the edge of the dance floor. She had stormed away while his buddies had grabbed him and taken him away to cool off and get high. She was still gone when he returned, but he didn't worry about it and went and got himself another beer. Likely she was just going to the bathroom or complaining to some of her girlfriends about him. It was a beer or two later before he realized that she had not returned and bleary thought took hold in his mind that he should go after her, though he knew he was in no state to calm any waters.

It was after eleven by then and the darkness away from the dance was near absolute with only the dim stars and moon above and the blinking lights of the nearby town offering any guidance. How the hell had people gotten around before electricity, he wondered to himself as he stumbled his way through the RV park by feel and hazy memory. He managed to avoid nearly every obstacle, but for a bush growing on the side of the trail that he wandered into, and found Emma's trailer.

"Emma, you there," he called out as he came to the door. He waited a moment for her to answer. When none came he swore under his breath and heaved a sigh before pulling open the door and climbing within. For a moment he was too occupied with finding the light switch to listen, but after he failed in that endeavor he stopped his fumbling and in the moment that he was standing still in the darkness he heard it. There was a man's whisper and a woman's soft laughter and then the rhythmic sound of their weight against the mattress.

He did not stay to hear any more, the door crashing shut behind him as he fled from the trailer, going headlong into the iron fire pit at the center of the campsite. It sent him sprawling to the ground, but he sprung back to his feet almost as soon as he had fallen, not even pausing to see if he was hurt. No sound followed in his wake, but he still kept turning back to see if Emma was rushing after him to stop his flight. No one was there but for he and the shadows.

Returning to the dance he found Colton and pulled him aside. His friend looked at him curiously an odd smile on his face. Dane's own face felt hot, as though all the turbulent feeling within him was erupting on his cheeks and forehead. For a moment he was worried that he would start to cry, but the emotion turned to anger in an instant and he grabbed Colton by the shoulder.

"Come on," he said, "We're going to Rimbey."

"What the hell man? Tonight?"

"Fuck yes."

Colton studied him a moment attempting to judge the level of his seriousness. At last he shook his head, "Come on man. I'm having a good time here. Let's just stick around till morning."

Dane felt the flush growing deeper on his face. "No, I'm going now."

"What the hell happened?" Dane didn't answer and Colton shook his head. "How much you had to drink? Neither of us is good to drive."

"I'm good," Dane said, not even convincing himself. "Look, I'm going right now. You can come or you can try to catch a ride with someone else tomorrow. It's my truck."

Colton considered this a moment, a wave of thoughts illuminating his face. At last he relented and they left the dance, Colton taking their last tickets to get some beer, which he smuggled out in his jacket. Dane was already at the truck, the engine idling. Dane took the beer Colton passed him, draining half of it in a single pull and then set it in the cup holder. He gripped the steering wheel tight but made no move to shift it into gear, a pensive look crossing his face. Colton was staring at him, a concerned look on his face, but he did not notice. At last, a decision made, he reached out and put the truck into gear and pulled out of the rodeo ground and onto the road.

2

The empty cans of beer had joined the other detritus on the floor of the truck, gathered over the past weeks of endless travel, a rodeo nearly every day. There were empty bags of chips and chocolate bar wrappers, bottles of Orange Crush half filled with Copenhagen spit, unopened packets of mustard and ketchup, along with napkins and coffee stir sticks and the other accouterments of a life on the road. Emma had always complained about the smell of the truck, but Dane and Colton no longer noticed. They spent so long in there, days and nights crossing the Canadian prairie and down into Montana and Wyoming and further south on the rodeo circuit, that the state of the vehicle had simply become normal to them both, as natural as the vast open expanses they drove through.

They drove in an uneasy silence, Colton glancing over from time to time at Dane, who did not take his eyes from the road. He stuck to the back roads and secondary highways, though it would add time to their journey, but there was little chance of their meeting a cop on patrol. They encountered no one as they went and after a time Dane put the truck in the middle of the road so that the headlights illuminated both ditches. The only other lights came from the farms and ranches they passed by, flickering beacons in the darkness.

They stopped once to take a leak on the side of highway, each of them instantly surrounded by a swarm of mosquitoes and bugs. Colton looked at Dane sideways as they stood there. At last, judging that enough time had passed to cool his friend's temper Colton spoke.

"What the hell is going on man?"

Dane zipped up his pants and walked towards the truck, not looking at Colton. "It's nothing. It's Emma is all."

"Bullshit nothing. Christ, why are we running around in the middle of the night then?"

Dane got in the truck without another word and Colton followed. "Get the stuff. I need a hit."

"You sure man?" Colton said and Dane glared at him. Colton reached for the glove compartment, clicking it open and rummaging through the papers within. "This doesn't seem like the best idea if we're driving."

"I'm tired man, I need to focus."

"Well I could drive for a while."

"Just get the shit," Dane said.

"Alright, alright. Calm down now," Colton said, retrieving a baggie and pipe. While he put some of the crystal in the pipe, Dane rolled down the windows, looking out morosely at the night.

They took a couple of hits each and then sat in silence as the high washed over them.

"Emma was with another guy," Dane said at last.

"Holy shit," Colton said, coughing. "You saw her?"

"Yeah," Dane said slowly, taking another hit. "Yeah. Couldn't find her. Went to look for her and she was in the trailer with this dude."

"Man," Colton said, returning the pipe and the baggie to their spots in the glove compartment. "Can't believe she'd do that. What'd you say to them?"

"Nothing. I just walked in and heard them in the back

and bailed. Didn't trust myself, you know."

Colton reflected on this for a moment. "So you didn't see her?"

Dane looked at him. "Pretty obvious what was going on man."

"I was just thinking, maybe it was Marcie, right? Could have been her too. They came together right?"

Dane worked at his lower lip with his teeth. "Nah, nah it was her. Where else was she, right?"

Colton nodded, "Yeah I guess."

Neither of them said anymore and Dane put the truck back on the road. They were flying soon, the darkness beyond the headlights seeming almost to blur as they passed by. Colton glanced over at the speedometer and then at Dane but said nothing, though he shifted uneasily in his seat. Dane slowed down when he had to turn on Highway 21 for a few miles, though it was as empty as all the other roads they had been on. He kept the truck in the middle of the road, drifting every now and again to one side or the other so that his tires ran across the warning strip at the center line, which shook the whole truck with a droning vibration.

He kept the truck there even as a pair of lights from a semi-truck blinked beyond a pair of hills in the distance. The lights disappeared, reappearing a moment later as the semi went down one hill and started over the next. They disappeared again as their own truck started up a steep hill, the engine working hard, and then appeared in a blinding flash atop the hill as the semi came down upon them. Dane flinched at the lights but made no move to pull the truck into the right lane.

"Hey man," Colton said, in a quiet voice that barely sounded over rumble of the straining engine. Dane gave no sign that he had heard, or that he noticed when the trucker sounded his horn and flashed his lights as the two vehicles moved perilously near, one upon the other. Only at the last moment, the semi nearly upon them, the horn sounding louder and louder did he pull the truck over and out of the way. The semi hurtled by, its passage shaking the truck so violently that Dane momentarily lost control of the vehicle.

"Fuck me man," Colton said after a few moments.

"What?"

"I think maybe I should drive."

"No," Dane said, as he turned off of 21 and onto the 570. The tires squealed as he made the corner and started to speed up again.

"I don't get it man," Colton said with a shake of his head. "You're losing your shit over a girl for fuck's sake. So she cheated on you. You either dump her or you live with it. Either way you move on, you don't go fucking batshit."

"Like you know shit about women, man."

"I know she's way the fuck out your league."

Dane slammed his fist on the dashboard. "Yeah, yeah. That's right. Way the fuck out of my league. That's the fucking problem right there. This is a goddamn game too her, this whole thing. You and me, we don't get day money, we don't fucking eat. She and Carl, they just call Daddy."

Colton didn't say anything, reaching into his back pocket and snapping his can of Copenhagen before taking a dip.

"One of these days she'll get tired of this and then she'll go back home. Everything will work out just fine for her no matter what. It always does. Me, I gotta go crawling back to the padre."

Dane could feel his lower lip quivering with emotion and stopped talking, knowing if he wasn't careful he would start crying from rage and hurt.

Colton laughed under his breath, though he glanced at his friend. "Fucking sucks, no doubt."

"You don't know the half of it," Dane said. "If he knew what we were doing tonight he'd probably re-baptize me."

"You sure they can get the holy water close enough to you without it boiling or something."

"I just turn it to piss."

They drove for a time in silence, both of them watching the road. Dane had not spoken to his father in months, not since the last time he had been home. His father had refused to give him any more money, saying that if Dane wanted to continue with the rodeo circuit and the life he was leading on it he could do it on his own with no help from him. It was all Keith's fault really, he thought. They had grown up together and Keith's family had gone to his father's church. When they had first started going to amateur rodeos and the n later on the circuit their parents had insisted that they travel together. They had for a while, but Keith still prayed before each ride. He didn't chew and he didn't drink, didn't chase girls, and Dane did all those things. Soon enough they had fallen out and Keith had informed Dane's father just what his son was up to on the road.

Several arguments had followed, each time Dane returned home, his father insisting that he give up his ways and Dane refusing. For a time his mother had managed to convince his father to continue to give him some money to help him out when the day money didn't cover everything, but eventually some final line had been crossed and his father had refused to extend a further hand. He had not even told either of them about Emma, not that it mattered now.

"Yeah, I don't know how much longer I got man, quite honest," Colton said.

"Yeah," Dane said his voice dull.

"Got to grow up sometime, I guess. Dad wants me back home helping out and I don't know. Can't really fool myself anymore that I'm going to amount to something doing this."

"Yeah."

"Anyway."

Dane glanced down at the gauges and said, "We gotta get gas."

"There's that truck stop on the number one. It'll definitely be open still."

"Right," Dane said and at the next intersection he turned left heading west.

3

The truck stop was just off the Trans Canada highway, surrounded by gleaming lights perched high above on poles, standing sentinel against the night. There was a gas station and convenience store, along with an all-night diner and a rest-stop area where truckers could park their semis for the night. There were a half dozen or so semis behind the buildings and a couple of truckers having coffee in the diner, but no one was at the pumps as they pulled up.

Colton went in to the store to get them something to eat and drink while Dane pumped the gas. He watched, leaning against the truck, his hand squeezing the nozzle, as Colton grabbed a few bags of chips and two chocolate milks. Dane turned away and spat out the last of his chew as Colton headed towards the cashier to pay and then turned his attention back to the pump to watch the dollars rise. As the tank began to reach full he felt his adrenaline spark. Looking back at the store he saw Colton had left and was heading towards him, a plastic bag full of his purchases swinging in his hand.

"Fucking ready?" he said and Colton nodded, stepping up into the cab of the truck. Dane waited until he had shut the door and then wandered over from the gas tank to the cab, trying to look casual as he did so. He opened the door and hopped in, swinging the door shut and starting the engine all in a single motion. He shifted the truck into gear and then slammed on the gas. The truck lurched forward, tires screeching. The truck seemed not to move for a long, agonizing moment before the tires grabbed and they sped off, the back end of the truck weaving like a boat crashing against waves.

Dane let out a whoop. At the same moment Colton, who was looking out the back window, swore. Looking in the rearview mirror Dane could see why. Somehow, in his rush to make their escape good, he had forgotten to take the nozzle out of the tank and the hose had torn off at the pump and now trailed behind them. He shook his head and began to laugh, Colton joining him after a moment.

"Fucking ridiculous," he said.

He flew down the Trans Canada and took the first exit he came to, driving at least a mile before he pulled off to the side of the road to remove the nozzle and hose from the gas tank. He tossed it into the ditch and then searched the back of the truck for the cap to the tank. After a few frantic moments, images of police lights coming over the hills behind them clouding his head, he found it in amongst their gear bags. He snapped it back in place and returned to the cab at a run, his breath tight in his throat.

"Lucky, lucky," Colton said shaking his head.

"Fuckin' rights," Dane said, exhaling and putting the truck into gear.

He drove slower now, barely nudging over the speed limit as they made their way back to the 570, not wanting to draw any attention. They met a few cars and after each one passed Dane kept his eyes on his mirrors to be sure they did not turn around and start a pursuit. No doubt the gas station had called the RCMP and they would have someone looking for them, but he figured the odds were in their favor. Now that they were off the Trans Canada there was little chance of any police being on patrol nearby, and those odds would decrease even more once they reached the secondary highways and back roads. The only danger was if whoever was called into the gas station guessed right as to what direction they had gone and which exit they had taken.

That seemed unlikely though and the farther they went the more relaxed they both became, their adrenaline mixing with the booze and drugs to make them giddy. As Dane turned onto the 570 Colton reached into the glove department bringing out the baggie and the pipe.

"Let's hit this shit again," he said.

"Yeah."

They had each taken a hit, Dane rolling down his window to clear out the smoke from the cab, when a car's headlights came into view behind an upcoming hill. They both went still, Colton letting the lighter go dead in his hand, and waited as the car came over the hill and passed them, going fast. They both turned to the mirrors and watched as the car kept on, looking as though it were going to head out the other side of the valley. Dane had already started to exhale in relief when its brake lights flashed red. In an instant they were gone and its headlights were glaring in their mirrors as the car headed towards them. The long moan of the siren and the dance of the red lights followed. Dane slammed on the gas, jerking the truck from side to side in his excitement so that they nearly went into a skid while Colton swore.

"Fucking Christ. Pull over, we can't outrun them."

"We'll see," Dane said, biting his lip in concentration. As they came to an intersection with a range road he slammed on the brakes, turning wildly, the truck pulling as though it were about to flip on its side. Colton flew from his seat, hitting his head on the roof and landing more or less in Dane's lap. He lost his grip on the steering wheel as a result and the truck skidded along the gravel. Pushing Colton aside, Dane regained control and slammed on the gas, accelerating with the tires spinning and gravel flying.

Behind them he could see the police car make the turn in pursuit, gaining on them by the instant. They went up a small rise, which plateaued, only to reveal a large hill up ahead. The truck engine strained to keep the pace he demanded, the flashing red lights getting ever closer in the mirror. As soon as he reached the top of the hill Dane let off on the accelerator and took the truck off the road and into the ditch, the vehicle bouncing in the air, both their heads crashing into the roof. As the truck stabilized he accelerated again aiming between two posts on the fence that ran alongside the road, snapping the wires in an instant as he crashed through and into the pasture.

He did not slow down, though the truck seemed ready to shake apart as they bounced across the prairie. In the mirrors he could see the police car had turned to follow them but had halted in the ditch and was not moving.

"Fuck me," he said, "I think they high-centered themselves."

Colton laughed and, after a moment, Dane joined him. A thought struck him a moment later and reached over and flipped off the truck's headlights and began to angle their path until they were parallel with the road they had just fled. After a minute or so they came across a trail that wound through the pasture and he turned onto it, knowing he was unlikely to drive into too much danger if he stayed on it. The trail also had to lead to somewhere, hopefully to other side of the pasture and the township road that had to be running perpendicular to the one they had been on.

Colton was rubbing the back of his head where it had landed against the roof, muttering to himself. Dane's own head ached as well, it felt as though both halves of his jaw had been slammed together while he was biting down on a piece of concrete. In spite of that he felt giddy, their escape made good and he turned up the stereo which had continued to blare the same Pantera album for the last hour. He sang along, Colton joining in as he rolled down his window and, with a flourish, through the baggie and pipe out to be claimed by the prairie.

As he had hoped the trail led them to a Texas gate and an approach to the township road, which he turned on heading east again, moving fast. He took the next range road they passed and then turned again onto a township road and back again, angling them south and east. He half wondered if he should double back to ensure that he had really lost any pursuit, but decided against it. No need to get fancy, just get away. The tension that had been with him since they had left the gas station, since they had left the dance really, dissipated as the minutes rolled on, it was now past one in the morning. Colton had fallen asleep, his head pressed against the door window.

They were somewhere east of Drumheller, as near as he could reckon it, when the police found them again. He saw the high beams glare first, creeping over the hill he had just passed, and felt his stomach fall away. The car came into view a moment later and then the lights came on. He had already started accelerating, swearing and slamming his hand against the steering wheel. Colton jolted awake looked in the mirror and then at Dane and just shook his head.

"Man, just give it up. We got rid of the stuff. Maybe we can talk our way out of it."

Dane did not slacken his pace. "Talk our way out of it? How the fuck do you think we can do that?"

"Probably can't. It's not like we got any choice. They're gonna be looking for us everywhere now."

Dane didn't reply, his eyes on the road ahead. They were in the hills above the Red Deer River, the road winding back and forth around them, the curves and the grade getting steeper and steeper as they started to descend. He nearly lost control twice taking the corners, the tires skidding on the gravel. The lights behind them seemed to loom brighter every time he looked in the rearview mirror. Finally they came to a hill with a sign warning of sharp corners and a speed limit of thirty kilometers. The road wrapped around the hill, turning back on itself twice in hairpin turns.

He made the first turn, sliding out to the road's edge. A wooden fence for the guard rail was the only protection against the truck plunging off the side of the hill down to the valley below. The light from his beams did not show how far the drop was, for which he was glad as he entered the second hairpin, slowing down even further to make it. It was not enough, though, the back end of the truck swung out and off the road, smashing into the guard rail. Though he tried to turn against it, the rest of the truck went too, hurtling through the wooden fence and then down the hillside.

He did not remember the truck halting its descent, nor if he had done anything to stop it. His arm and leg ached, but otherwise he seemed to be fine. The engine had died so he tried to start it again, but it just turned over without catching. It was only then that he noticed that Colton was not sitting beside him and that the windshield was shattered.

"Fuck," he whispered to himself. He screamed as he tried to open the door, passing out again. When he came to he used his other arm and crawled out slowly, trying not to jar his broken arm in any way. His leg hurt to put weight on, but not as much as his arm, so he assumed it was not broken. He looked around in front of truck where the lights illuminated the grass and sage of the river valley for Colton but didn't see him. Turning back to the hill above he saw the police car, lights still flashing, sitting where he had gone through the rail and swore again. Turning away he limped off through the pasture and into the darkness.

4

There were words being spoken that Dane could not understand, as though they were being uttered from a great distance. He squinted at the sun's glare, the blue of the clear sky almost too bright to look at. Sweat trickled down his back but his feet were cold, the current of the river moving around him, the sensation making him lightheaded. He briefly wondered if he were about to faint and tried to focus on the assembled gathered on the bank of the river. His eyes found his mother's face and she smiled in encouragement

His father stood beside him, speaking to the congregation, all in suits and dresses somber in color, all staring back at him with expressions of gravity. His father frowned as he spoke, but that was normal, his voice shaking with emotion, which was not.

"Our Lord and Savior has blessed us, you, with this second chance," his father was saying, the rest drifting from his ears as if carried by the current below.

He felt numb listening to it. Before he would have smirked his way through the service, making plain his disdain for the ceremony and what it meant. Now he simply did not feel a part of it, did not feel a part of the anything and had not for a very long time. He was absent from the world and nothing that happened in it could matter to him. It had been that way since the night he never thought of, never spoke of, never dreamed of. Perhaps the living part of him, the spirit, had gone then, leaving only this flesh to remain, keeping his place.

"Have you, Dane Matierry, accepted Jesus Christ as your personal Savior and Lord?"

He turned to his father. "Yes, I have."

His father continued, "Because you have accepted Christ as your Savior and Lord, and because He commands that you be baptized, I baptize you, my son in the name of the Father and of the Son and of the Holy Spirit. Amen."

A hand was placed on the back of his neck, his father's, and he was lowered gently into the river. He looked up at the empty sky, the glorious shining blue, the water cool and quick against his body. His father lowered him deeper so that his entire head was submerged beneath the river's wash. For an exquisite moment he thought he was to stay there beneath the waters, never to return, but his father's hand guided up and out of the water and back into the world.

IT CAME FROM ABOVE

1

The object lay hidden in a small valley, near the dugout in the lease pasture, where water sometimes gathered in the spring. A scattered band of trees formed a loose semi-circle behind it, both crowning and hiding it, so that if Frank had come from another direction he likely would have missed it. He nearly did anyway, for it seemed to disappear in the moment it took him to register the oddity of the thing being there. It was only a tingling at the back of his neck that caused him to stop and turn to get a clear look and confirm that something was in fact there.

"What the hell," he muttered to himself and then turned down the radio. He stayed where he was for a long time, his lips pursed in thought, before shifting the truck back into gear and slowly making his way down towards it.

From a distance it had looked thick and square but as he drove nearer it seemed not to have any firm shape at all. Or, rather, it had many shapes, for it looked as though it were constantly altering its form, so quickly he could only just perceive it. The sensation made his eyes itch. It was as tall as he and perhaps as wide as the truck, with a deep velvety dark color, almost black, that seemed to absorb, not reflect, the day's sun. How that was possible he could not say, but nothing about it seemed to fit within the realm of his existence.

He pulled up beside it and got out to inspect it more closely. He walked around it twice, looking at it from all angles, gaining no further insight into its purpose or its origin. It seemed to be humming – the working of an internal engine? – at a frequency just beyond his hearing. Bracing himself, he reached out and touched it. The sensation was indescribable. A tingling, almost numbing, sensation ran up his arm to his shoulder. Instantly he jerked his hand away, holding it up before his eyes and turning it over and back. The feeling disappeared as soon as he removed it and there was no visible sign of anything wrong with his hand.

He touched the object again, wincing at the sensation, running his hand up and down the structure, feeling for the joints and screws that tied it all together. He found none. The whole thing felt unreal, as though his hand was sitting atop a pool of water, but when he pressed against the object he could not penetrate the surface to whatever depths lay within. Even as he had his hand pressed against it, the object continued its strange shifting, the almost subliminal movement that triggered some deep and instinctive response within him.

It was an hour or more later, after he had spent a great deal more time investigating the object, all to no purpose, that he reluctantly got back in his truck and started for home. What, he wondered, did he do about this?

2

Constable Jennings, the RCMP officer, was unable to disguise his disbelief at the site of the object.

"Well, I've got no clue," he said with a shake of his head.

Frank shook his head in agreement. "Gotta be like a UFO or whatever, right? Got to be."

Jennings gave a little shrug of his shoulders, as if he were not willing to venture just yet as to the nature of the thing, and started around it again, a frown on his face. Frank had called him out that morning, after spending an uneasy night trying to decide what to do. If it were a UFO, as he suspected, then he had to proceed very carefully, lest it be taken from him somehow. He wanted to make absolutely certain that he got whatever he could from finding it. It would be worth a dozen oil wells or a year's worth of testing by the Concern.

The constable finished his circle and returned to stand by Frank. "Like I say, I've got no idea."

"What do we do now?"

"Well, unless someone comes forward to claim it, I think it's yours to do as you please. I'll just ask around a bit and make sure nobody's space ship got away from them.

Other than that, I imagine there'll be a lot folks wanting a look at that thing."

"You mean the Concern," Frank said.

"How's that?"

"When you say you'll ask around, you mean the Concern."

Jennings nodded. "I don't know what they do in there."

"Nobody on this planet has built anything like this, I can guarantee you that," Frank said. Jennings shrugged and turned back to look at the thing one more time, running his hand along it and whistling at the sensation.

They both left the pasture at the same time, Frank trailing the constable's car, feeling uneasy. He was certain that the object was of alien origins, but all the same, he did not want the Concern involved. He did not trust them. That was why, in the end, he had called the RCMP before anyone else, so that at least things were official and on the record. If the object disappeared somehow in the coming days, then at least he had the police to turn to. They were not on the Concern's payroll, even if everyone else in town was.

He told Emma about it that night after she had put Colton to bed, showing her some pictures he'd taken with his cell phone. Even though he had been very careful with each attempt, none of the pictures were in focus.

"It's the strangest damn thing," he said to her.

She frowned. "I'd like to see it."

"We can head up tomorrow when you're back from school. I'm going to try to get some better pictures tomorrow and then send them to the Herald."

"Why the Herald? Why not the Echo?"

"This is not some small time story: Carol and the kids visiting Martha in Wainright, or whatever. This is big. It's going to change everything."

Emma nodded, though he could see doubt on her face.

"Someone will pay a mint for this," he said, "So long as the Concern doesn't get involved."

She sighed. "Why would they?"

"You just wait," he said. "You just wait. They'll try to claim it's theirs. They'll want to look at it, I guarantee it."

"I don't know why you're so worried about them."

"I don't trust them. Who knows what they're doing in the Baas."

Emma shook her head. "They've done a lot of good for this town. The school wouldn't be open, for one thing, if they hadn't brought so much work in. Where would we be then?"

He stopped himself from saying anything, recognizing the tone in her voice. He was in no mood for the longer, messier argument it always presaged. It always ended at the same place, regardless of where it started. Ever since Colton had been born, Emma had wanted to move closer to her parents in Medicine Hat. In the first years after his birth, when she could only get work as a substitute, it had been a daily topic of conversation. Her hiring as the seventh grade teacher – now the grade seven and eight teacher with the split classrooms – had placated her for the time being. But not forever, he knew.

Rather than stir old wounds he went down to the basement and caught the end of the baseball game and drank a few beers. By the time he returned upstairs Emma had gone to bed and the house was dark and quiet.

3

Jennings called the next day and asked him to take him to the object that morning. Frank agreed, with some trepidation, wondering why the constable needed to see it so soon again. After he had done the chores he drove up to the lease pasture, which was about half an hour north of the home quarter. The last mile was on a dirt road which was badly rutted from the rains the week before and all the subsequent traffic had only worsened its state.

When he reached the pasture gate the constable was waiting for him, along with a picker truck and two men he didn't recognize. Jennings had an unreadable expression on his face as Frank pulled alongside his car, while the two men looked bored as they leaned against the picker talking to each other.

"What the hell's this?" Frank said, not even bothering to get out of the truck.

"These boys are here to pick up that thing. It apparently has an owner."

"Who?" he asked, though he knew the answer without it being said.

"Concern. Talked to them last night and they said they'd been missing a prototype for the last week."

"That right."

"Yeah. 'Fraid so."

Frank shook his head. "They say how it got here?"

Jennings walked over and leaned against the truck, giving him a sympathetic look. "No. Couldn't understand it. Didn't know where it had gone at all apparently. They were thinking someone had stolen it."

"They report it to you guys."

Jennings shook his head. "They were treating it as an internal matter."

"I bet," Frank said and then jerked his head at the two men by the truck. "Who are these guys?"

"Picker truck they brought in from Hanna apparently. They're going to take it over to the Baas."

Frank looked them both over, his eyes hard, and one of them nodded in acknowledgment. He responded in kind before turning back to Jennings. "I got to tell you, I don't see any reason why I should have to turn this over to them."

"Now don't be that way Frank. It's certainly isn't yours, unless you've been up to a lot more than raising Herefords."

"Well, how do we know it's theirs? They give you any proof of ownership?"

"Come on Frank," Jennings said. "Let's not make a big deal out of this. You had to know there was a pretty good chance it was theirs. They do a lot research at the Baas. This is from one of the projects."

"They told you that."

"They did. And a good deal more, which I'm not at liberty to talk about. Satisfied me anyway. You don't have much of a claim to the thing. I'm sure they'll compensate you for the trouble and having the picker truck out in the lease. But that's that, as far as I'm concerned."

Frank didn't respond, looking off into the distance at the rolling pasture and the cloudless sky.

"Come on," Jennings said. "I'd like to get this taken

care of this morning, if I can."

After a moment Frank returned his gaze to the constable and nodded. He got out of the truck and opened the gate waving the picker truck and Jennings by. After closing the gate behind them, he drove out ahead and led them down the trail to where the object lay. It was still there, unchanged from before, as impenetrably mysterious as when he had first set eyes on it.

The two men in the picker truck studied it for a few moments, shaking their heads and chatting back and forth. Frank half-listened to them, his thoughts elsewhere and his answers monosyllabic. When they had satisfied their curiosity the two men set about tying straps to the thing, a difficult task given its block-like nature, for the picker to be able to lift with. That done one of them worked the picker, while the other guided the object to the vehicle's flat deck. When they had it loaded and tied down Frank led them back through the pasture and then followed them down the road.

As they came to his home quarter he did not turn off, continuing down to the highway, where he watched as both the truck and the squad car turned west. He stayed at the intersection watching until the object, looking even more alien beneath the straps they had used to tie it down, disappeared from view.

4

Over the next week Frank was unable to chase thoughts of the object from his mind. The day Jennings and the others took it he returned to the pasture to inspect the ground where it had lain, but only the crushed and yellowing grass indicated anything had ever been there. He began to find reasons to head into town on errands just so that he could drive by the Baas, as if he could somehow peer behind the concrete walls of the old pig barns to see whatever the Concern was doing within. In town he contrived to run into people who worked at the Baas to see if they knew anything about the object that had been discovered at his place. Many had heard about it – the whole town seemed to know – but few had seen it or could tell him anything that he didn't already know.

"They probably didn't bring it back to the Baas," the night watchmen Arnold told him. "If something was going on with it, then they would have taken it up to Edmonton to have the folks there look at it."

"What's going on there really?" Frank asked him in hushed voice, as though he were worried about someone overhearing them.

Arnold shrugged and glanced at the grocery store

where he was headed. "You know, I couldn't really tell you Frank. I just watch the place. They don't really like me wandering around too much."

He excused himself and went on to the store, leaving Frank nodding to himself as though all his suspicions had been confirmed.

The Concern had come to town ten years before, about the same time Frank had married Emma, a godsend for a town like theirs in the lost quarter of Alberta where towns had been declining and disappearing for years with the oil and gas reserves that had fed so many nearing depletion. Farming and ranching still kept on as always, but there were fewer and fewer who remained on larger and larger tracts of land, with the result that the supporting infrastructure in towns – schools, hospitals, and stores – could no longer maintain itself on the few who were left.

The Concern had inserted itself into this situation, made more desperate by the threat of the closure of the town's school, with the offer of jobs and newcomers, the lifeblood of any small town. It had all been too perfect, for the failed Baas hog project had left three massive unused pig barns that the Concern could convert into space for its projects. What these were exactly remained murky, at least to those who didn't work there. Government contracts it was said. Security clearances were required for everyone, even those from town, and nobody could access the structures without permission and an escort. All very unusual in this part of the world where no one bothered locking their doors.

Now that they had the object Frank knew that he would never see it again, yet that did not stop him from trying to figure out what had happened to it. When one of the Concern's managers, David Hildeck, stopped by to pay his compensation for finding the object he pressed him to no avail.

"Damndest thing I've ever seen. Didn't even look like something from this planet, you know."

"Hm. Yes, it's a fairly bleeding edge prototype as I understand these things. It's not really my department though."

"Bleeding edge. I'd say. How the hell did it wander out of the Baas?"

"As I understand the design team had taken it out for some testing. We have a section of land where not far from your property there."

"Ryan's old hay field."

"That's correct."

"Bit of a waste of a hay field, don't you think?"

David frowned. "From the agriculture perspective of course it is a waste of good land. It suits our purposes though."

Frank smiled allowing some venom to creep into his voice. "Yes, I suppose so."

David steered the conversation back towards the compensation, rattling off the set rates the Concern paid for access to the land with heavy equipment. Frank agreed with his offer, which was more than generous as always. When the Concern had first moved into town everyone had been amazed at how much they were willing to spend on any little thing like access or renting the most basic of equipment. More money than sense, Frank had always said, but like everyone else he had never complained about being on the receiving end of it.

When everything had been settled and Hildeck made to go, Frank tried again to shake loose some information. "So what's that thing do anyway that it could get away from you like that?"

"That's not something I'm able to discuss unfortunately," David said, smiling slightly. "As I said, it's not really my area of expertise."

"Of course, of course," Frank said. "I understand. I just can't figure how it managed to get out in my pasture."

"Well, the test was obviously less of a success than the design team would have preferred."

"Back to the drawing board then."

"Yes, I guess so," David said and then thanked him for his help in recovering the object. Frank smiled and told him it was nothing. He watched the Concern man head out of the yard and down the road, thinking that he knew a bullshitting politician when he met one and David Hildeck was a bullshitter supreme.

5

Frank's suspicions about the object and the Concern only continued to fester in the days that followed Hildeck's visit. He was certain the man was lying to him. What kind of manager didn't know what projects were going on in his own company? He went online and tried to do a search on the kinds of work the Concern did, but there was little to be found. It seemed as though the company had erased all traces of itself, beyond a basic website filled with profiles of smiling employees talking about the benefits of working for the company and all the opportunities afforded them. There were a few vague sounding statements that made up their mission and vision, all of which seemed like only so much more bullshit to Frank. They were hiding something, no doubt.

No one could tell him that the object had been something they had built. It was like nothing he had ever seen, with a purpose beyond anything he could comprehend. He was not the sort of person to believe in aliens or ghosts or anything like that, but he had seen the thing, had felt it, and there was no doubt in his mind that no man had crafted it. It seemed clear to him what had happened. When Jennings had gone to talk with the

Concern they had of course said that they were missing an object just like the one he had described to them. Of course they had wanted to get their hands on it, to study it, to profit from it.

His continued obsession exasperated Emma to no end, but he could not help himself, even as he could see her anger towards him building. In some strange way it satisfied him to have her share in his wretchedness, even if he was the cause of hers.

"If I have to hear one more goddamn time about that thing," Emma said to him after four days, "It's done. Let it go."

He couldn't, though he knew there was nothing to be done about it now that the Concern had the object. But it was not fair to her and it was too much to bear in a year when so many things had gone wrong. Emma had not been happy coming here, but she had done so for him, even though it meant being four hours from her parents and most of her friends. She had made a life for herself, made new friends, made do, all for him. And she was, he thought, willing to stay if that was what he wanted, if it made him happy.

But with the Concern and these last terrible years he had not been happy. Nothing was as it had been when he had been growing up; his parents had even left, retiring to Calgary to be closer to his sister and her children. And through it all Emma wondered why he would not leave, if the thing he had did not make him happy, why not leave it for a new life. He could not explain to her, no matter how he tried, that it was simply not in him to.

A windstorm struck the following day compounding their shared misery. The air was filled with the remnants of the parched and eroding topsoil, so much that he could barely see the road from their porch. In the few minutes he spent outside, moving between the shop, his truck, and the house, his eyes and mouth filled with grit. It was impossible to do anything, impossible to go anywhere so both he and Emma were forced to spend the day indoors, each upon the others heels. Denied the comfort of their usual routine and worried about what was happening to the crops and the garden with the unrelenting wind their nerves frayed and they found themselves snapping at each other.

"Why don't you play with Colton?" Emma said at last as the boy asked them again why he couldn't go outside to play. "You hardly ever have the chance this time of year to spend any time with him."

Frank rubbed his eyes in exasperation, the house rumbling and echoing under the punishment of the wind, sounding at moments as though it might fly apart.

"Fine," he said, spitting the words out.

They played Fish and Snakes and Ladders, until his restlessness got the better of him and he left for the shop, aimlessly tinkering at a few projects he had started last winter. By the time he returned to the house for supper the wind showed no signs of abating and even after they had gone to bed it continued to howl and shake the house. He and Emma lay beside one another unable to sleep, listening to the house sound of its disenchantment.

"Tomorrow I'm gonna go in and talk to someone at the Concern," Frank said, closing his eyes and able only to see the wind and the dust buffeting the house, sounding like his own gritted teeth.

Emma sighed. "Why would you want to bother?"

"If this is some top secret project then they can pay me some more money to keep my mouth shut. And if it's not, then I think I should get the thing back."

"To do what?"

"To sell to the highest bidder," he said, rolling onto his side, trying to peer through the darkness to make out the expression on her face. He could feel her anger from where he lay, yet he could not stop his compulsion to explain this to her. He could feel his face go flush with embarrassment that he was forcing them both to talk about this again, especially since he knew what it would lead to.

"I just don't understand why you can't let this go."

"Why should I?" he said, as though the very thought were an affront. "That money could really help us. It's going to be a tough year."

She was quiet for a bit and he knew what was coming next. "Maybe instead of pinning your hopes on some crazy plan you could think about what Dad offered. We'd have some security. You'd know what hours you'd be working and we'd be closer to Medicine Hat."

"You think I'm crazy? You saw the pictures, you don't think that thing wasn't alien?"

She sighed. "That's not the point. I have no idea what it was, but what is the most logical explanation for it?"

He lay on his back trying to control his emotions, hating himself for all of this. "If you'd felt it."

"Jennings felt it didn't he?" she interrupted him. "And he thought it was from the Concern."

He didn't answer, staring off into the darkness. Emma reached across to grasp his shoulder. "Frank," she said, "I don't want to talk about this anymore. You believe what you want, but I'm done hearing about it. Okay?"

"Okay. I'm still gonna go tomorrow. Can't hurt."

He could feel the shake of her head. "Well maybe I'll go to see Mom and Dad tomorrow. And I'll see when I come back."

"Don't be like that," he said, trying to keep his tone even.

"Don't tell me what to do. Not when you're being like this."

She rolled over, turning her back to him, signaling the end of their discussion for the night and even he was not fool enough to say anything further. Better to let her have the last word, he told himself, especially when she was right. Beside him he heard Emma's breathing deepen and he felt the tension at last ebb out of him. Sleep eluded him though, and he stared up wide eyed into the darkness, his mind filled with images of the object and men from the Concern hunched over it trying to pry open its mysteries.

6

The wind did not begin to subside until late the next evening and it was not until the following morning that they awoke to a day glorious and calm. He had work to do around the yard in the morning, chores and repairs on one of the tractors, so it was only after lunch that he left, telling Emma that he was going up to check on the water at the lease. The dugout there had been low the day the object had been taken and there had been no rain since.

Though Emma had given him a look as though she suspected he were up to something, he had no intention of confronting the Concern about the object. He had thought about it the night after their argument and throughout the next day and had decided against it. He knew Emma well enough to understand which of her threats she would make good on. Stubborn as he was, even he could recognize that the object was not something that was worth risking his marriage.

The aftereffects of the storm were evident everywhere as he drove north. Ditches were filled with drifts of a fine powdery earth, almost like sand and several of his neighbors' yards had trees that had been uprooted. There was a grain bin lying crumpled and warped atop Werner's hill, an amazing site, for the nearest bins that could have been carried here were at Barthels, over two miles away. None of the power lines were damaged, as far as he could see, which told him that it had been blown high enough to clear them. The fences along the road were all filled with detritus, anything that hadn't been weighted down had been scattered across the country.

The dugout in the lease was as low as he could remember it being. Two cows were standing right at its center with water up to their waists when he drove up. Unless it rained in the next few days he would be trucking water up here by next week. He swore to himself thinking of how much time that would take. Three quarters of an hour each way, with half an hour to fill up the water tank. Two trips every other day. That would be three mornings gone a week at least, to say nothing of Tommy's pasture, which he would be hauling water to soon enough as well.

He was about to head home, his head filled with worry for what the rest of the summer would bring, when the ground where the object had been caught his eye. The grass had not recovered at all, had in fact turned a brittle shade of brown. It cracked underneath his feet as he walked across it, and each step was marked with the outlines of footprints. He could feel the color go from his face and he crouched down, as much to steady himself as to inspect the grass. He prodded the individual strands delicately with his fingers and they crumbled to dust at his touch. Cursing under his breath, he pulled the knife from the front pocket of his jeans and dug into the ground to expose the roots below. They too were utterly desiccated.

He said nothing when he returned home for supper, though he could feel Emma's watchful eye upon him. They went to bed wordless and he again found himself staring at the ceiling waiting for sleep to steal him from his thoughts. That night it would not though. Try as he might he could not forget the ruined, brown patch. Would anything grow there again? And was the object having the same unseen effect upon him even as he lay there? It was a terrifying thought to say the least.

The next morning he awoke tired and with an aching head. His jaw had been clenched tight through his fitful sleep, his anger not dissipating, even through his tumultuous dreams. He drank his coffee and had his porridge in silence, Emma watching him as she ate her toast. When he was done he pushed aside his plate and his cup and stared at her. Their eyes held for a moment and then she closed her eyes, warding herself for a blow.

"I'm going to the Concern today. That fucking thing killed a bunch of grass up in the lease. They're going to have pay for it."

Emma offered no reply, her face impassive, as he left the house, letting the door slam in his wake.

He went into town after he was finished with the chores, getting some parts at the Agro Centre. On his way back he turned off the highway and headed down the road to the Baas. The three long barns loomed up before him, still the same white they had been when the Dutch company had been running pigs there. A chain link fence surrounded the yard now, which also had a dozen or so trailers near its entrance that acted as offices for the Concern employees. The trailers formed a sort of informal blockade between the gate and the barns where the research was done. There was also a small hut at the entrance where everyone had to check in before being allowed into the compound and Frank stopped there, asking to speak with Hildeck. He was sent to the largest trailer where he found the manager and a young woman he did not recognize.

"Frank, this is Katy Miles. She's actually working on the project that, uh, you encountered," Hildeck said as he motioned for him to sit.

Frank stared at her fiercely, derision and rage written plainly on his face, so that Hildeck cleared his throat and motioned for her to leave, which she did, her face flooding with relief. "What can I do for you Frank?"

"That fucking project of yours is killing my grass."

David frowned and leaned forward. "How do you mean?"

"Where it was, all the grass is dead. The roots are dead. It's not coming back."

"Well," Hildeck said, leaning back in his chair, "That is strange."

"That's one goddamn word for it alright," Frank said. "I touched the thing. What the hell is it going to do to me?"

David started up, as though he had been awoken from his thoughts, and waved his hand. "Oh, it's been fully tested. We have people working with it all the time. No long term effects have been observed."

"I bet."

"I wonder if we could get a look at that grass though. It might help the team get a handle on what happened there."

Frank smirked and took off his ballcap, running a hand through his hair. "You don't have a clue what happened do you?"

"Well, I certainly don't. It's a little outside my expertise."

"Not a clue at all," Frank continued, ignoring Hildeck. "You know what the thing is supposed to do?"

"I'm afraid I can't really discuss that, you understand. We have certain security protocols," Hildeck said, shifting uncomfortably in his chair. "Now, to get back to your pasture, we'd certainly like to get a look at that. Can we discuss getting access? We'll gladly pay of course."

"I know you will."

David cleared his throat. "Well then. I'm sure we can come to some sort of agreement."

"I'd like to see the thing again."

"The prototype?"

"Yes," Frank said leaning forward in his chair for

emphasis.

"I'm afraid that's impossible. We have protocols and I don't think I can get permission. We'll gladly pay our standard access fees. And of course for the damage the prototype did."

Frank did not reply, standing up and walking out the door, leaving Hildeck to stare after him in disbelief. He got in his truck, spinning out as he turned around to head back out to the road, slinging gravel across the yard. He flew home, pushing the needle to 160 kilometers, oblivious of the other traffic on the highway. The radio was on but he talked over it, cursing Hildeck and the Concern for stealing the object, and Jennings for letting them. It was clear to him now that they had no more idea of what the thing did than he.

When he pulled into the yard he saw that Emma's car was gone. He sat in the truck for a moment unable to quite process what he was seeing and then ran inside, calling her name. There was no answer and as he looked through the living room he saw that all of Colton's toys were gone. There was a note on the kitchen table that read: *I've gone to Mom and Dad's for a few days .I'll call on Saturday and we can talk*. He slumped into a chair holding the note up and looking at the words, not reading any of them.

7

That night, unable to stand being in the house, where the silence cried out his shame, a moment longer, he fled back to town heading to the hotel for a drink. He slid onto a stool at the bar, not even looking to see if there was anyone he knew in the place, and ordered a Pilsner. The first two beers he drank without noticing he had done so, unable to escape the cloud of his thoughts. They alternated between rage at the Concern and what they had done and disgust at himself for his own stupidity. How did he convince Emma to return now? She would not get back together with him unless he agreed to leave for Medicine Hat, not after the past week, not after today. He did not have that in him.

The fog of the beer washed over his gloom and it was some time before he emerged and was aware of what was occurring around him. He heard a woman's voice behind him and turned to see Katy Miles sitting with another woman at a table. Their eyes met and her smile vanished as she studied him warily. Noticing her gaze her friend turned to look at Frank and offered him a bold grin.

"Hey, what's your name?" the friend said ignoring the look Katy shot her.

"Frank," he said, stepping away from the bar to join them.

"I'm Lisa and this is Katy," she said, extending a hand to him.

"We've had the pleasure," Katy said, frowning at Lisa. "Frank is the one who found the prototype on his land."

"Oh," she said, the light going out of her voice a bit. She recovered though, leaning towards Frank conspiratorially, "Must seem like quite the mystery."

"It does that," he said.

"Well, it's pretty boring I can tell you. I never understand why we have to have all this secrecy. I mean, what would you do with that information? Nothing, it doesn't matter at all to you."

"Well, it matters a bit," he said. "That damn thing killed the grass in my pasture."

"Really," Katy said leaning forward in her chair and exchanging a glance with Lisa.

"Hildeck didn't tell you?"

"No," Lisa made a face.

"He never tells us anything unless we absolutely need to know it. I hardly know what the prototype is and I work on it. Or one part of it anyway."

"It's weird," Lisa agreed.

"How can you work on something when you don't know what it does?" he asked them as the waitress came by with another round of beers.

They both shrugged and Katy said, "It's like we're dealing with a series of connected problems right. But each problem is its own thing and has to be solved on its own. So maybe you need to know a little about one or two problems to solve your own, but only a few people need to solve the whole equation."

Frank nodded as though he understood, but he had lost the train of her thought about halfway through her speech. The room spun as he looked away from the two of them and it took him a moment to bring everything back into focus. Lisa had already shifted the topic away from the object and was talking about how strange it was to be living in such a small town so far from everything. He nodded and listened to her, answering both their questions about his own life, how he had grown up here and what he thought about living out here. It was hard to explain these things, especially after he'd had as many beers as he had, but he had never really considered any other kind of life. Their lives were the foreign ones and it was incomprehensible to him that anyone would choose differently than he had, given the choice.

After an hour or so Katy left and he and Lisa stayed drinking and talking. He could not recall anything they said, even a moment later, the world blurring at its edges. It was dangerous, though, he knew that much. He had not taken a good look at everyone who had been in the bar that night, but most of them would know him and would know that she was not his wife. It would be talked about. And if it was talked about then Emma was guaranteed to hear about it in some form or another at some point. His worry and fear at what he was doing dimmed as the night went on though, and they left together, Lisa taking him outside by the hand, both of them laughing and drunk. They stopped by his truck and he reached into his pocket for his keys, but she stopped him with a hand on his arm.

"You shouldn't drive," she said. "Not after all we've had to drink. Why don't you come back to my place? It's not that far a walk."

He found this amusing for some reason, because nowhere in this town was a far walk and yet no one except kids too young to have vehicles walked anywhere.

"What's so funny?" she said, giving him a playful shove, which he returned. She turned her face up to kiss him and he leaned down, their lips meeting haphazardly. He could feel her smiling as they kissed and a current ran through him, stronger even than the haze of the beer, as he pressed her up against his truck. They separated and he stepped back from her, their eyes never leaving one another.

"Are you coming?" she said with a smile, holding out her hand.

He considered the hand for a moment and then shook his head abruptly. "No, I got to go."

Without looking at her again, for he dared not, he got into the truck and left, tires screeching and rubber burning.

8

He stayed to the back roads to avoid the police, shouting at himself as he drove. As soon as he sat at that table he should have known that woman was trouble. It had been obvious, but he hadn't cared until it was too late. Worst of all he couldn't get the smell of her out of his nose, or the feel of her mouth and her breasts from his mind. Each time he thought of her he hated himself more, but his loathing only spurred his thoughts of the two of them pressed against his truck.

Had anyone seen them? Who had been in the bar that night and had seen them leave together? He might as well have just gone home with her, enjoyed the night, because the stories would tell it that way and Emma would never believe otherwise. What had he done lately to prove himself worthy of her trust after all?

As he drove past the Baas he looked at the barns, illuminated by the yard lights, posted like sentinels along the fence surrounding it. The only other light to be seen was in the shack by the entrance where Arnold would be sitting, a quarter of the way through his bottle of rye. He drove on for a mile and then turned around and headed back, thinking that maybe he could salvage something from this mess of an evening.

The shack door opened up and Arnold stepped out to see who it was as he pulled up to the locked gate. Frank gave what he thought was a jaunty wave and rolled down his window and Arnold came alongside the truck.

"What's up Frank?" he said, eyeing him cautiously.

"Oh, nothing Arnold. Just heading back from town, thought I'd stop by."

"That right?"

"Yeah, I was thinking maybe you could show me around. I'd sure like to get a look at that thing they found at my place again."

Arnold frowned. "You know I can't do that Frank. Christ, I'd lose my job. They got cameras everywhere."

"You just switch out the tapes. Don't you ever watch the movies? They do stuff like that all the time."

Arnold shook his head and turned to go back to the shack. "Can't you at least spare a little rye? It's a long drive home," Frank called after him.

Arnold turned around and said, "Sounds like you've had more than enough to get you there."

He went into the shack and Frank got out of the truck and followed after him. "Come on Arnold. What the hell?"

"Christ Frank, you could get me fired."

"Hasn't stopped you yet."

Arnold shot him a look and gritted his teeth. For a second Frank thought the night watchman was going to punch him, but instead he reached into his desk and pulled out the bottle of Alberta Premium. He poured a bit into the coffee cup on his desk and then passed the bottle over to Frank who took a long swig.

"Thanks," he said. "What the hell do you do all night?"

Arnold gestured at the table which was filled with crossword puzzle and Sudoku books. Frank took another swig of whiskey and then set the bottle on the table and grabbed one of the books. He flipped through the pages looking at the puzzles hazily and then threw the book back on the table. Arnold frowned and returned the book to its proper alignment.

"Never could get into those things," Frank said.

"You should try them. Give you something to think about."

"I got enough on my mind as it is."

"Well, maybe this would help get your mind off of things."

Frank nodded as though he were considering this. The whiskey seemed to send the world spinning and for a moment he was worried that he would pass out right there. He shook himself back to alertness and saw Arnold frowning at him and pursing his lips. This made him angry for some reason. That a goddamn drunk like Arnold should be judging him. He stood up to go, wavering for a moment as the world lost and then regained its equilibrium.

"Well," he said with a shrug, "Fuck it."

He reached down to grab the bottle and then brought it up as though to take one last swig, but instead he twisted it around in his hand and, leaning across the table, swung it down on Arnold's head. It shattered and Arnold shouted in surprise and jumped to his feet, grabbing at his eyes, and stumbling against his desk. One punch knocked him off his feet and the second knocked him out. Frank gave him a third for good measure, immediately regretting it as the impact of Arnold's head against the concrete floor made a sickening sound. Frank blinked in surprise at it and tried to feel for a pulse. He failed in that attempt and placed a hand on his chest to see if he still had a heartbeat, only to realize Arnold was still breathing.

That worry quelled for the moment, he fumbled at Arnold's belt for the keys to the Baas and let himself in through the gate. He went to the nearest barn and after three tries found the right key and opened the door. As soon as he stepped within the alarm started to sound, a deafening squawk, and he nearly jumped back outside. He tried the keypad to the right of the door, punching in numbers to no effect. Ignoring the alarm, he flicked on the lights and stepped from the entryway down a short hallway, off of which were a few small offices and a break room. The hallway ended at another locked doorway. He found the key for that as well and went on.

The interior the building was little changed from its time as a pig barn, they had just emptied the guts of the thing out leaving walls and floors bare of pens and crates. There were a few dim walking lights on above, providing just enough light so that he could make his way through without stumbling. The room was filled with scattered workstations and equipment he vaguely recognized, saws and welders, but industrial-type models he assumed. There were various pieces of things on tables, awaiting assembly or construction presumably, and they looked like parts for a machine, though what kind of apparatus he couldn't fathom.

The next two rooms were much the same and he didn't linger, the alarm mixed with the alcohol giving him a terrible headache. The final room was locked as well and he fumbled with keys in his excitement, knowing somehow that this was the place he had been looking for. At last he found the key and sent the door thudding open against the wall. The sound echoed through the room. He walked in and stopped, sure that he had seen something move, but everything appeared still. The eerie sensation of a thing there and not there immediately overwhelmed him and for a second his eyes could not focus. When they did he nearly fell to his knees.

There were dozens of the things, all more or less the same size as the one he had found, of indeterminate form and use. They seemed to hum at the same frequency just beyond his hearing, speaking to each other. He walked among them and could almost imagine how they would join together to create something massive, the size of house perhaps. The thought left him dazed. He started to reach out to touch one of them but then stopped himself. It was suddenly very difficult for him to breath and he left the room, going back through the building the way he had come, slowly at first and then at a run.

He emerged from the building in time to see the police car pull up beside his truck. Jennings stepped out and looked around and Frank began to walk towards him.

THE DANE

1

Nels bellied up to the bar, pushing past two young bucks. He shouted to Harold for a beer, slapping his hand on the table. "Goddamn Harry. Goddamn."

"You're hot as a poker," Harold said, grinning as he filled a mug with lager. He handed it across the counter to Nels. "What's got you fired up anyway?"

"Today is a red letter day, my friend. My wallet is full and I am going to drink my fill. That I guarantee." He spoke with the faintest of Nordic accents, that the few Swedes in the area found unplaceable. They had never met a Dane from Slesvig, as he was quick to say.

"Good for you, Nels," Harry said, reaching across to give him a slap on the shoulder.

Nels nodded his thanks and took a long pull on his beer, wiping the suds from his mustache. He was well known in Sunnynook, but then everyone was. It was a homesteaders town of about a couple hundred, bigger than most of the others in the area because it was on the railway and had a station house and an elevator. Farmers from thirty miles or more would bring their grain and cattle here to ship and sell.

That was what Nels had been doing as well, selling his

cattle, to somebody down near Hanna. *For a hell of price*, as he kept thinking to himself, while he slapped the counter of the bar in rhythm to a song that only he could hear in his head. If harvest went off half as well as the cattle, well he'd be looking at his first great year here in the five since he'd settled.

He was a latecomer, compared to most everyone else. Most of the families had been settled here fifteen or twenty years. They'd built up their lands—or in the case of a good many, failed and buggered off somewhere else— and turned their sod shacks into sturdy houses. Nels was still working on that.

He was only one man himself, so he only needed one room, as he always said. And the cold of the Canadian prairie wasn't so bad. No worse than his winters in Denmark. The damp there got into you worse, he told everyone. Went right to the bone and you couldn't get it out, no matter what you did.

Not that he wouldn't mind one of those catalog houses, ordered up and the plans and pieces sent in on the train. And if this year went like he thought it might...well, hell, he might be building next summer.

He finished off the last of his beer and waved at Harold for another, just as Wally Lindback tapped him on the shoulder. Nels turned to look him over and shook his hand. "What are you doing here, boy? Aren't you too young to be in a place like this?"

"Dad would kill me if he found out," Wally said, with an agreeable shrug.

Nels laughed. "I'll spot you a beer."

"Thanks," Wally said. "Saves me asking. You seem flush tonight."

"Been a hell of day, Wally. Hell of a day. Sold the cattle. Got a fine, fine price, I don't mind telling you."

"That's great. And you got that crop coming too."

"Still have ta get it off," Nels said, though his grin said he thought that would be no problem. He waved the bartender over and ordered a beer for Wally and another for himself.

"Dad's still broken up about his," Wally said, a shadow passing across his face.

Nels frowned. "Yeah, that's a hell of thing. That's farming though. And he's not the only one. Hail took a lot of good crops this year. Not mine for once though, not mine."

Harold brought the two beer over and Nels passed one on to Wally, peeling off some bills to pay the tab. He raised his glass and Wally followed suit.

"Yeah," Wally said, taking a sip of his beer while he looked past Nels at the others in the bar. "I wouldn't maybe go telling everybody about your good fortune. They're liable to get jealous."

"Oh folks here are good," Nels said, unconcerned. "Most are good farmers like your dad. They understand that some years will be good, some bad. You learn to roll with what life gives you. Can't do otherwise."

"Yeah," Wally said, taking another drink. "Yeah." But he did not appear to believe it.

2

The sun was low on the horizon, turning the sky blood red and golden, and the clouds a deep violet, when the two men exited the hotel and went to the stables for their horses. Nels had spotted Wally another beer, having another two himself, and he looked at the younger man with the blossoming warmth the alcohol provided him. He was a good lad, Nels thought, if a trifle morose. But, then, he had been the same at his age, and more liable to find himself in trouble.

They headed north out of town on the main road. Nels' place was about a mile north and another mile west on the township line, while Wally and his family lived a quarter mile north of the township line. They were among Nels' closest neighbors, especially in the last few years, after the bad harvests, when so many of the latest wave of homesteaders had given up and abandoned their quarter sections.

Nels had given consideration to the idea as well. Many would have, unwilling to live the miserable kind of existence he had these last five years. For a time it had seemed nothing could go right. His crops had failed—even his gardens had been pathetic, but that had just been inexperience—and he had spent the winters with hardly any food and no money to buy more, or to pay for coal or wood to heat the place. Oh, it had been a mean life, make no mistake, but all that would be over now, after this year.

They rode in silence for the first half mile, the horses ambling slowly, as if they did not want to return home. At length, Nels spoke, the good cheer brought on by his fine day and the beer, putting him in an expansive mood.

"You know how much your dad meant to me these past few years?" When Wally didn't respond, he continued. "Helped me out so often, I can't ever repay the debt. Hell of a thing. Sometimes I think everything I know about farming I learned from him. Definitely wouldn't be having the success I'm having now without him."

For some reason the praise of his father seemed to darken Wally's mood. His lips curled and looked away from Nels, off into the gloaming air.

Nels, in his general good cheer, did not notice. "Hell of a sunset tonight. Have your folk's heard from Anne?"

Wally's sister Anne had gone to Normal School in Saskatoon two weeks earlier, so that she could become a school teacher, something sure to be in high demand in Sunnynook in the coming years.

Wally shrugged. "Yeah. She's settled in, I guess." He turned to study Nels through narrowed eyes. "You made out well with the cattle, huh? I was telling Dad we should get into them more. He didn't listen. Would be nice to have that money now."

Nels waved a happy, dismissive hand. "Oh, it was good this year. But who knows about the next. Besides, your folks can survive one bad year. It won't get so lean for you as it was for me, that's for damn sure. Your mom and dad already went through that when you were young."

"Yeah," Wally said, not sounding as though he believed it.

They lapsed into silence again until they came near the township line, where they would part ways, Nels turning west and Wally carrying on north.

"How much you make from those cows anyway?" Wally said, his voice strained and quick. "If you don't mind my asking," he added, unwilling to look in Nels' direction.

Nels pulled his horse to a halt and stared at the younger man. "Now, what might be on your mind, young man?"

Noticing that Nels had stopped, Wally pulled his horse around, still refusing to meet the other man's eyes. "Nothing," he said. "Just talking."

"That wasn't talk, son."

Wally glanced over his shoulder, as if hoping for someone to appear to stop this confrontation. "It was nothing, really. Let's just head on our way. Dad'll be wondering where I am."

"I'm wondering myself," Nels said, making no move.

Wally sighed. "It's just...I need money."

"That so. You haven't talked to your dad?"

"No," Wally said, with some vehemence, before stopping himself from saying anymore.

"Out with it," Nels said.

Wally looked as though he wanted to turn his horse and gallop away as fast as possible. "All right. It's about a girl."

Nels was unable to hide a smile. "Which one?"

"Agnes Miller."

"Sure."

Wally sighed. "I want to marry her, but Dad doesn't think it's a good idea."

"But you're gonna do it anyway."

"Yeah," Wally said defiantly.

Nels laughed. "Oh, I had a burr under my ass too, when I was your age. Got myself into a lot more trouble than you, I expect. Let me tell you something about your mom and dad. My first two years here, I didn't have any crops. No money. Nothing. You know, I wouldn't have hacked it, if not for your parents. You know why?"

Wally shook his head.

"Because they gave me food. They gave me seed for my crops for the next year, when I didn't have enough to plant. If not for them, who knows where I'd be. Your parents are some of the kindest people I know. You just have to remember that. They'll come around on Agnes, whatever they say. They probably think you're too young and this is too soon?"

Wally nodded.

"Yeah. Well getting hitched yourself will only make them sure of it. I know it feels like forever, but you just gotta be patient for a bit. I wish I'd had somebody tell me that when I was your age. They'll come around."

Wally looked as though he didn't agree, but he nodded.

"Get on home now," Nels said. "And come and talk to me before you do anything too damned foolish."

They parted ways, Nels heading west, looking up into the dying light of the day. The shadows hung heavy over the prairie, but the horse, well-used to this route, loped easily along the trail, knowing that it was nearing home. There was only a thin line of red along the horizon, reflecting off the alkali slough that lay just to the northwest of his house, when Nels arrived. He was still smiling about young Walter when he came into his house and saw the dim forms of two men waiting for him in the shadows.

3

Nels stopped still in the doorway, his grin vanishing and his whole body going tense. One man sat at the table, while the other loomed behind over near the stove.

"Hullo Daniel," the man at the table said. He turned up the lantern sitting near his elbow, casting a meager bit of light about the room, and gestured for Nels to join him.

Nels looked from the man at the table—his face clearly visible, the ugly scar across his nose very memorable—to the man by the stove, still obscured by shadows, the light of the lantern not reaching there. Neither man moved. Nels stepped across the threshold, a decision made, and sat across from the scarred man.

"I'm afraid you got the wrong fellow," he said, holding out his hands apologetically. "My name's not Daniel. It's Nels Sletkolem."

"So you say." The scarred man looked from Nels to his partner. "We heard that too. That you go by Nels here. A Dane. Talk to any Swede though and they'll say they don't know any Dane talks like you. Isn't that right Eddie?"

The man in the shadows grunted his agreement. Whether his form in shadows revealed it or some instinct told him, Nels knew the man was holding a pistol, aimed at him. Beads of sweat formed on his lip, though it was cool in the house with the sun gone.

"I don't know what to tell you boys. I'm not who you're looking for. Whatever you, and whatever some Swedes, might think."

The scarred man's lips curled into a faint grin. He pulled a gun from within the coat he wore and set it on the table. "You see this here Daniel?" He gestured to his nose. The scar ran along the bridge, across and down, to where most of his left nostril should have been. "You don't forget this, right? No one would. Especially not when they're the one who did it.

"And let me tell you," the scarred man continued. "I wouldn't forget the face of the man who did it to me. Or his name. I wouldn't forget you, Daniel."

"We've been looking for you a long time, Daniel," the man called Eddie said.

Nels drew in his breath, looking from one to the other. "Well, I'm sorry to disappoint you. But I don't know either of you. I don't know what you're talking about. I'd appreciate if you kindly went on your way. I've got an early morning tomorrow."

"What kind of fool do you think I am, Daniel? This song and dance may have worked on the Irish. He's not the curious sort. Me, I get the answers I want. One way or another.." He gestured at the revolver on the table.

Nels wet his lips. It was clear that it didn't matter what he told the intruders, they would not believe him. And they were undoubtedly here to kill him. This was all just a prelude to that. The answers the scarred man wanted, whatever they might be, would not stop him from pulling the trigger. There was no road that did not lead there, which meant Nels would have to see if he could somehow not start down it.

That would be the trick. There was no one near enough to help. Wright Arnold and his family were the closest to Nels homestead, a quarter mile away. They would probably hear the shots. But, in the unlikely event they decided gunshots were worthy of investigation, these two would be far enough away it wouldn't matter.

Nels cleared his throat and looked at the scarred man, giving him a helpless shrug. "What do you want, then?"

"So you admit who you are? You admit what you did?"

Nels studied the scarred man. If he moved quickly, he figured he had an even chance of getting his pistol, which still sat on the table. But it would be a near thing, not at all clean, and there was Eddie, standing in the shadows, to think about. Not good odds, but maybe the best he would get.

He had a .22 rifle and a shotgun, both hanging over the door. At least that was where he'd put them. These two men might have been here waiting for him for some time though, and they seemed the sort to notice two guns hanging above a doorway. Besides which, they were not loaded, and the shells were on the shelf behind Eddie.

He held his hands out. "I don't know what you're talking about, like I said. If it's money you're wanting—"

"You know what the hell I want, Daniel." The scarred man slammed his fist on the table, causing the lantern to list to the side, ready to topple.

By reflex he reached out to right it and Nels saw his chance. He leapt across the table and had the scarred man's gun in his grasp before he could react. But he was not quick enough. Eddie moved out of the shadows, even as Nels stretched across the table. He brought the butt of his pistol down onto Nels' temple, sending him to the floor, along with the scarred man's gun, which clattered away.

There was fumbling and cursing in the dim light, but at the end of it all the two men had their guns and Nels was sitting on the floor with an aching head.

4

The scarred man sat back down at the table, gesturing for Eddie to stay near Nels. He pushed his hat back on his head and glared down. "I'm getting mighty tired of your nonsense here. Admit what you did Daniel."

"Why don't we just plug him?" Eddie said, his looming presence casting Nels in shadow. He had a square face and small sinister eyes that made his expression ugly.

"He's going to goddamn admit what he did."

Nels looked up at Eddie. "He needs me to admit it because he's not sure himself. You talk to anyone in this town, they know who I am. Nels Sletkolem. I don't know who this Daniel is, or how long ago all that was. But he doesn't know for a certainty."

"Don't play games with me, Daniel," the scarred man said. "Quit stalling. Eddie here can convince you to talk if need be."

"He doesn't know for certain," Nels said, speaking with a confidence he did not possess.

A flicker of doubt crossed Eddie's face and he glanced at the scarred man. "Are you sure Connie? We could just plug him and be on our way."

Connie slammed his fist against table. "Don't listen to

him Eddie. Damnit, this is the man who cut me up. I don't forget faces. I sure as hell don't forget that face."

"It was a long time ago," Eddie said.

"Not that long."

Eddie shrugged and looked back at Nels. "What does it matter then if he talks or not? Let's plug the bastard."

"It matters, Eddie, because he's going to admit what he did before he dies. He's going to admit what he did and die with the knowledge that he paid for what he did to me. He's going to go to his grave knowing that he answered for the wrong he did."

"Okay," Eddie said, though it did not appear that he understood the scarred man's reasoning.

"Perhaps you can illuminate me as to what I've done," Nels said, rubbing his head, which ached where Eddie struck him with the butt of the gun. "That way I can confess better. Because I gotta be honest, I don't have a damn clue what you're blathering on about, but I'm sure getting tired of hearing about it."

Connie stiffened. "Hit the bastard for me," he said to Eddie, who shrugged and obliged.

Nels groaned as Eddie's large paw connected with his nose. He could feel the bone give way beneath the weight of the blow and felt a trickle of blood run down his lips to his chin and the floor.

"You're a big man, Constance, sending others to fight your battles. If I did you so wrong, why don't you get your hands dirty? I bet this guy doesn't even know what I'm so guilty of, but you'll let him carry a murder rap for it and sell him down the river the first chance you get."

Eddie shot Connie a suspicious glance and Nels smiled, knowing he had struck a nerve.

The scarred man was apoplectic. "What in God's name are you listening to him for Eddie? He's been a liar every damn day of his life. A liar and a cheat."

"What did he do Connie? Really?" Eddie said.

"He did this," Connie said, pointing at his nose. "That

would be enough. And he stole a score off me and the Irish and left me to take the fall. It's damn rich that he's saying I would do the same to you."

"I don't know what he's talking about," Nels said to Eddie. "I'm not this guy Daniel. I've never seen this fellow and his ugly nose before."

Connie let out a shout of uncontrolled rage and leapt out of his chair coming across the room toward Nels. This time he sent the lantern flying off the table. It landed on the floor, the glass shattering and oil spilling outward, and, with it, the fire within. The floor, bult from thin boards, repurposed from an old wagon, went up like kindling wherever the oil and flame touched.

Eddie shouted in fear at the sight of the conflagration and started toward it, intending to stamp it out. He collided with Connie, on his way to take Nels by the throat, and the two men fell to the floor in a tangle of limbs. They fought against each other to get back to their feet, each desperate to reach their goal, each thwarting the other in the attempt.

Nels did not hesitate. He was on his feet, ignoring the wave of pain and the blurring in his vision from the blows to his head. Taking one of the chairs from the table, he brought it down on Eddie's head, who let out an odd grunt and slumped to the floor. Connie, who was trapped beneath the larger man, cursed and struggled to move his huge frame, now limp and nearly immovable.

Nels did not wait to see if he would succeed. He ran out the door and into the darkness, heading to the northwest toward the alkali slough.

5

Connie managed to work himself free of Eddie's body and stumbled outside. He blinked at the darkness, which was now near total, only the moon, thin and new above, providing any illumination. The fire soon would, for it was spreading up the table and toward the nearest wall and would soon reach the stove.

For a moment, he thought of Eddie, unconscious and certain to be consumed by the flames and he hesitated. As he did he saw a flash of motion, the hint of a form, heading toward the lake north of the house. His rage overcame him and he ran, snarling, in that direction, his hands balled into fists.

He ran until the ground became uneven and he nearly stumbled fell. From there he had to proceed more carefully, alert for any changes to the shadows that surrounded him. The house popped and hissed behind him, making it difficult for Connie to hear if anyone was approaching. But he felt certain no one was. Daniel had run before to this godforsaken place at the ends of the earth, and he was running now.

If this was really Daniel, but he was certain it was. Accent or no. Time had changed how he looked, but not so much that Connie didn't recognize the man who had ruined his face.

The thought of that, and the realization that he might be running again, made him bold and he threw caution to the wind, yelling out at the darkness. "Come out you bastard. You can't hide from what you did. You knew I'd find you eventually. I did. And I will again. You can't escape this."

There was no response and he came to a halt, listening to his own breathing. Behind him the roof on the house collapsed, the fire surging into the night air, as though it was taking its own heavy breaths. Connie jumped back away from the fire by instinct, though he was far from it now, and found himself slipping and nearly falling down a steep incline, suggesting the lake was near.

Connie recovered his balance, looking around wildly, in case Daniel took this opportunity to attack. There was no movement nearby and he allowed himself to relax, his confidence returning. Daniel or Nels or whatever the hell he wanted to call himself, had always been yellow and always would be. He would always be running.

"This is what you are, Daniel," he couldn't resist yelling out over the roar of the fire. "Yellow and running. Well you run. I'll damn well find you."

He spared a glance at the house, which seemed near immolation, and felt a pang of guilt for leaving Eddie to his fate there. A damn shame, he told himself, but the clumsy bastard shouldn't have got in the way. Worst of all, he had allowed Daniel to escape, which meant that Connie would have to start tracking him all over again. He would do that gladly, he would do whatever was necessary to see this to its end. The Irish would have questions, but he always did, and Connie was tired of them anyway.

He decided to return to the barn, which now seemed dangerously close to the burning house. The horse and buggy he and Eddie had procured earlier in the day at the next town over were tucked in behind it and he couldn't afford to have them running off. Now that he thought about it, it was surprising they hadn't already.

Maybe that's where Daniel had gone. Though that didn't really seem like Daniel, not the man he remembered anyway, in spite of all he had said. That man, he was forced to admit, would stay and see this night through to whatever end was coming. The last time that had left Connie with a wrecked face and an anger that could never be extinguished.

He had just taken a step toward the barn, when he heard a sound behind him. Something like a splash of water, but not quite, muffled but very near. Sensing his moment of triumph was at hand, Connie leapt in the direction of the sound, his teeth bared.

He expected to plunge into the shallows of the lake, but instead he stood on solid ground. Or ground that was solid for a moment, but soon gave way. He tried to get out, to go forward, or back, but the more he moved the further he sank, the mud of the alkali pulling him deeper and deeper.

As he tried to yank one of his legs free and keep his balance, Daniel appeared at his side, startling and sending Connie to one knee.

"Not used to an alkali slough are we?" Nels said.

Why was he still going on with that accent, Connie wondered. "You were always a goddamn coward."

"I don't know what you're talking about," Nels said. "All I know is I wouldn't have left my friend in there to die."

"You sonofabitch," Connie said, jerking his hand free and reaching into his coat for his gun.

It wasn't there. Startled, he looked around, thinking he had dropped it in the slough. But he hadn't. He had left it on the table when he had taken Daniel's bait and gotten tangled up with Eddie. Left it there when he ran out of the house, after Daniel, into the night. Now the fire had it.

He looked behind at this man, whose fearsome

expression was dimly visible through the light of the moon and the fire. Was he really Daniel or Nels? Now, in this moment, doubt for the first time crept through. His face wasn't quite what Daniel's had been. How were these Swedes to know whether his accent was right or not?

Connie screamed, rage and fear and agony all wrapped up in one, as the man seized him by the head and brought a knife to his throat and cut it away.

6

Nels held on to Connie's head as he choked and spat blood, moaning unintelligibly. It spurted from the gash in his neck, regular as a heart beat, gradually slowing as the life went from him. Only when his body was nearly limp, almost falling anyway, did Nels release him and let him fall into the slough.

He looked down, cleaning off his knife and shook his head. "I always wondered if I would have been better just finishing what I had started," he said, with no trace of a Danish accent in his voice.

Shaking his head, he turned back to the house, which still burned steadily. The barn was safe just yet. Lucky it was a calm night and it had rained recently. Lucky for a lot of reasons, Daniel thought to himself.

He shrugged and headed up to the barn, leading the buggy and horse Connie and Eddie had brought with them away from the fire and tied them to a fencepost on the corral on the other side of the barn. That reminded him of the cattle he had just sold and the money tucked into the pocket over his breast. He shook his head in irritation.

Heading back to the barn, he let out his own horses, just in case the fire happened to spread. One of the neighbors would find them and keep them. He retrieved a shovel from the barn and went back down to the alkali slough and started to dig by the light of the fire and the moon, carving a trench big enough to hold the body.

When he was satisfied, he used the shovel to push Connie into it and then covered the body over with mud. He smoothed it as best he could, knowing that the alkali would settle and its surface would appear untouched in a day or too. Sooner if it rained. He just had to hope the coyotes didn't get to the body in the meantime, or that whoever came across his place, burned to the ground, didn't get too curious.

His luck would hold again, for the smoke from the fire was mostly dissipated by morning, and it was two days before someone happened by and saw the burned out house. It was Wally Lindback who came by, hoping to chat with Nels more about his father and Agnes Miller. Wally rushed into the house and saw the burned and shriveled corpse, rendered unrecognizable and assumed the worst

There was an investigation eventually, the RCMP arriving two days later. By then, Connie's body had disappeared into the depths of the slough. Not that it mattered, no one wandered out that way. Both Wally and Harry mentioned how Nels had been talking all night about the money he had earned from his cattle. It seemed obvious to everyone what had happened.

All of that Daniel was unaware of as he put whatever he thought was worth taking from the barn into the buggy. Dawn was beginning to creep over the horizon by the time he was ready to go. He took one last look at the smoldering ruins before climbing up into the buggy seat and setting out to begin again.

SMEAGOL BLUES

David could remember, with exact precision, the moment he became aware of the house. His mother had been going into town to run some errands and had taken both he and his brother Eric along for the ride. It was the year before she fell ill, the last time that he would see her as she had been, not as what she would become in those agonizing final years. He would have been seven years old. It was early July, the grass still bright and green from the June rains. He had seen it a hundred times or more of course, for they passed it every time they went into town. He was always left to wonder why, in that moment, it had seized him.

It was known as the Faulkenbourg Place after the Swede who had homesteaded the quarter. He had ordered the house from a catalogue for a couple of hundred dollars in the early twenties, a prefab from the Canadian Aladdin Company, their Edmonton model. In David's memory the house always had the same ramshackle look to it, in need of a coat of paint, the same remnants of past owners littering the surrounding yard, and the grass overgrown around it. That was how it looked in that moment, and later, through all the changes, the coats of paint and trees planted, the new roof, when the image of it came to his mind it would be of that first moment of awareness.

There was no sense to his fascination, both then and later, it was simply a thing that existed within him which he did not question. He wanted to see the house up close, to feel what it was like to be within its confines and to know all that there was about it. That such a foreign entity, for it seemed very alien to him, could inhabit a space so near the familiar of his home, just a mile down the road, was part of its appeal. His world was very small then: the farm yard, the lands his father owned, the town, and the roads taken to visit these places. All were infinitely and reassuringly familiar. The house was something else entirely, standing apart from all he knew.

The next year his father purchased the quarter the house was on and his summer was spent in, what he conceived as, a grand adventure of discovery. His father wanted the house fixed up for a farm hand he was planning on bringing on for the harvest that fall, so the entire family was enlisted in whatever spare moments could be found to tame the abandoned yard and paint and repair the house. For David each moment offered the thrill of the new. There were the overgrown remnants of an abandoned root cellar, here the rusting spine of a broken plow, and, leaning against the back of the house, a lone wagon wheel.

The interior of the house, the source of much intricate and fevered imagining on his part, was the true find though. For once reality lived up to dream. The floors creaked ominously with each step, threatening, in his mind, to splinter and collapse, releasing whatever fearsome and hidden things had been trapped beneath it. The smell of decay hung foully in the air, made visible in the bird and mouse droppings in the corners and along the walls. His mother, her face with that strained and waxy pallor he would come to know so well, declared that the place would never lose the smell of this. David hoped that she was right, that the place would be abandoned again and become his secret alone.

That proved an impossible dream, at least for the moment, as by summer's end the house fairly shone with new paint in and out. A cat and some mousetraps had removed the rodents, for the most part, and regular tending of the yard made the whole place look like any other farm yard that David passed on his way to town. That fall, as planned, his father hired a man to help with the harvest and he moved into the house. From that time on it was well-kept and occupied, though David could still recall the alluring decay, the sense of absence that had drawn him in as though he might somehow inhabit it.

It was during that fall that his mother's illness became inescapably apparent to David, the strange pallor that he had noticed that summer now a permanent feature of her face. There were other changes as well, though little noticed by him. His mother was always tired, often going to bed early in the evening when he and Eric did, and on particularly bad mornings it was their father who would rouse them get their breakfasts and send them off to the bus for school. Sometimes their usual after supper games, crib and rummy and kings on the corner, would be left to he and Eric alone.

The dim concern David felt for these developments, more a sense that this was unusual than any true understanding of what they implied, was offset by the arrival of harvest. It was his favorite time of the year, filled with bustle and activity, given greater meaning by the race to get the crop off before the weather turned. This year his excitement was magnified by the addition to the proceedings of the new farm hand, a fellow named Jim from Enchant.

The farm hand and his father worked from dawn till dusk, so long as the weather held and there was wheat to harvest. When David came home from school he would take the two lunch pails his mother had prepared, full of sandwiches, sliced cucumber and tomatoes with some cookies for desert, and two thermoses full of tea out to the grain bins where Jim was unloading the truck. Jim would give him a ride out to the field, keeping up a friendly chatter that to David's ears sounded worldly and wise, and then David would run one of the pails and a thermos over to the tractor and combine his father was driving.

He would sit beside his father, nestled precariously on the armrest, with the various unfathomable gear sticks threatening to jab him in the back, as he made his rounds in the field and ate his supper. He enjoyed watching the swath disappearing into the combine, transformed into kernels of wheat straw that would be spit out the back of the machine. His father did not really say anything in these moments, focused on his supper and the task at hand, but David did not mind. It was enough to watch, to hear the throttle of tractor and the rumble of the combine as they worked. Sometimes, if his father allowed it, he would stay out on the tractor until his eyes grew too heavy and then Jim would take him home for bed.

On the weekends they would all eat lunch in the fields, sitting in lawn chairs out on the stubble in the shadow of the machinery. The talk would be on the progress of the harvest, how this field was going tougher than the last, how the equipment was holding up, and how the weather might threaten or bless in the days to come. David would listen to these conversations with fascination, feeling a part of some monumental task, the import of which he could not quite grasp.

One day, Jim seemingly tired of all the talk of work, asked about the Faulkenbourg Place.

"Why do they call it that?" he wanted to know.

His father finished the bread he was eating and said, "Albert Faulkenbourg homesteaded that quarter. He bought the house and put it up there in twenty two or twenty three I think."

177

"What happened to him? Get moved out in the Thirties?"

"No. The year after he built it he was killed. He was disking a field and something spooked his team. He was thrown off his seat and the discer went right over him. Dad found him the next day."

"That's a hard thing."

"Yes it was."

"Your family bought it after that?"

"No, it went through a few hands," here his father paused tantalizingly, as though there were much more to be said. "Bit of a bad luck place I guess you could say. Land's a bit sandy too."

Jim stayed on through the winter and into the next fall as well. During the summer, when more of his time was his own and he had much more freedom to navigate, David would often make his way over to the Faulkenbourg Place to chat with the farm hand, who didn't seem to mind the company. He taught David how to throw a proper curveball and told him about the time he had batted against Satchel Paige when the Negro Leaguers were barnstorming through Saskatchewan.

As much as he enjoyed the Jim's company, the larger purpose of his visits was to be within the house. It was a compulsion, deeper than any understanding he was capable of. The thrill he felt as he stepped from the entryway, to the kitchen or the living room, to sit across from Jim and talk was something near ecstasy, especially now that he knew what had happened to Albert Faulkenbourg. To be in these same places where a dead man had sat and done the same things he had was an incomprehensible and new thing to David.

Jim left in the middle of the next winter, a particularly harsh one, even by the standards of the Canadian prairies. The first snow had fallen a week after Thanksgiving and stayed on through November and into the new year, accumulating into vast drifts that hardened into immovable dunes, reshaping the landscape entirely. The drifts in the yard were so large and solid that the cattle could walk out of their pens and the tractors were unable to break through them. The temperature offered no reprieve, staying well below freezing so that even the slightest breeze was cutting.

It was in January, when the days were at their shortest, the sun setting before five, making the cold seem to set in the bone all the more, that Jim came by their house to announce his leaving. David was at the kitchen table playing cards with his mother while his father finished his tea and read the paper. Jim looked sheepish as he unbundled himself on the porch and apologized for disturbing their evening. His father waved away his concerns and poured them both a glass of whiskey. They retired to the living room to talk.

Though David made a great show of playing his hands, he lost three games in a row as he tried to play and listen to what was being said in the living room between the two men.

"I'm just here to give my notice," Jim was saying. "Sorry to spring it on you like this."

"You've got something else then?" his father said, in that even tone he used to indicate disapproval.

"No, not exactly yet." Here Jim stammered. "I know some folks in Maidstone."

There was a pause where David could imagine his father taking a measure of the situation while he took a sip of his whiskey. "Is there a problem, something you're not telling me?" he said. "I think I've been fair in all our dealings. I could understand if you had something better lined up. Lord knows you don't want to be doing this your whole life."

Jim's discomfort was plain in the way he spoke. "It's not anything you've done. You've done right by me Walter. I can't thank you enough for the opportunity. Just time to move on I guess."

"There's not something else wrong is there?"

"No, no," Jim said and there was a long silence. "It's the house, if I'm being honest. There's something about it doesn't sit right."

"How do you mean?" his father said, sounding confused.

"I can't explain it really. I just don't feel right in it, like there's something else there with me."

"A ghost you mean?"

"No. I know what you're thinking. Jim's gone crazy. I swear to you, it's nothing like that. I can't explain it. I know there's nothing there. Can't be. But it just doesn't feel right."

They left it at that, his father thanking him for his help and wishing him the best. Later David would overhear him talking about the situation with his mother, saying that maybe it was a blessing that he had gone when he had. "He can't be right in the head, thinking there's something in that house with him. Who ever heard of such a thing?"

David knew what Jim had tried and failed to tell his father, that sensation that escaped all words yet sunk deep into the center of his being never to be shaken free. Jim had been afraid of it, though he had tried to hide it in front of his father. David, though, felt no fear, only a longing that somehow he imagined would be made whole by the place itself and whatever lay within.

There were several hired men who passed through the Faulkenburg Place in the following years. None of them stayed for long, though none admitted to feeling any odd sensations while living in the house. It was the nature of job that there would be so much overturn, at least that was what David's father told him. At the same time the farm prospered and, along with the rest of their neighbors, their family had money to spend. They put electricity and plumbing in the house not long after, removing the last vestiges of its homesteader roots.

What truly marked the passage of time though was the worsening of his mother's condition. There was the day when she ceased to rise to see he and Eric off in the morning, the day when his father started to make their suppers after he came in from work, the day when she could no longer walk without help, and, worst of all, the day when he had to keep score in their nightly game of gin rummy. Though it was never said by anyone, David understand that these were the way stations on the path to oblivion, that his mother was dying, as Albert Faulkenbourg had died, as the steers did when they were sent to market in the fall.

Death did not seem a strange occurrence to him, not when he was surrounded by it daily. He assisted in killing the hens and pigs when the time came each year and had spent many an afternoon watching hawks lazily circling the sky above a tractor as it moved through the field, stirring up the mice and voles below. This, he understood, was a different kind of death, a momentous one, the others merely profane. It wasn't the fact of the death that told him this, dying seemed much the same regardless of who or what was doing it, it was everyone else's reactions to it.

Visitors that came to the farm, even the various hired men, would speak in hushed tones or with a forced joviality when his mother was about, her condition obvious at a glance. They would not meet her eyes and then stare at her when they thought she wasn't looking. David suspected she noticed it all, though she never said. His father, taciturn by nature, turned ever more inward as his mother's condition worsened, some days speaking no more than a dozen words. Eric, too, retreated within himself, passing his hours at home in his room, not even spending time with David. He was hurt by this change in his brother, for in their younger days they had been inseparable.

Unlike the others, David was drawn to his mother, spending as much time as he could with her. He became the one who unfailingly helped her around the house as that became more difficult. He found reasons to be near her, to touch her, crawling into her lap to sit, though she found such contact painful in her condition. His father would yell at him to leave her be when he would see him sitting in her arms and he would slink away, only to return later as soon as his father had gone away. The smell of her fascinated him, musty and rank, as though an unseen decay had already begun within her. As the end neared and she spent more and more time in bed, neither sleeping nor truly awake, David would secrete himself in the hall outside her bedroom and stay for hours listening to her labored breathing.

He was fourteen when death granted her the peace life had not. Just as her illness had changed and reordered the cosmos of the farm, so her passing did again. His father withdrew ever more inward, working blindly in the fields, and in the evenings retreating to his office or to shop, where he would tinker mindlessly on some project or another. It fell to Eric to take care of them, once the neighboring wives stopped bringing over meals they had prepared, getting David up in the morning for school, helping him with his lunch and making supper for them when they got home. It was a role he resented for the burden it placed upon him, and yet fiercely protected whenever David would try to care for himself.

For his part, David felt lost in this new world, so he avoided both his father and brother as much as he could. He would wander among the three rows of trees, evergreens and caraganas, which divided the farm from the road, playing in imagined realms in the shade of the branches. Days when he knew the farm hand was out working or in town, he would take his bike and ride the mile to the Faulkenbourg Place, sitting in one of the rooms on the floor, staring off into nothing. In those long hours he felt it speak to him, its soundless reverberations echoing through the center of his being.

Even as he turned fifteen and started high school, a time when he knew he should have moved beyond these childish things, he continued to venture to the house, its very presence reassuring him. One Sunday, with his father and brother having retreated into their respective worlds and the farm hand gone home for the weekend, he went over to pass the dreary afternoon. He stayed for hours, losing track of time, watching the sun move through the sky by the changing light coming through the windows. Though he knew he should leave, that the farm hand would be returning soon, he could not bring himself to stir from his reverie, until he heard the truck wheels on the driveway.

In an instant he was on his feet, sweat on his forehead and panic in his mind. He stayed frozen for a moment, unsure of what to do, knowing only that he couldn't go out the front door without being seen. The windows were no good either. He would need time to get their screens off and their being open would be evidence enough of his presence. Had he been a little older and a little more confident he might have met Grant at the door with an apology and some excuse – no butter in the house – which he would likely have accepted without question.

Unable to think of anything else, he fled to the bathroom, climbing into the tub and ducking down so that his head did not peek over the side. This proved to be a poor hiding place, for after the long drive from Bonneyville, the first thing the farm hand did was go to the bathroom. He had his fly unzipped before he noticed David.

"Goddamn Christ," he said with a jump. For a terrifying moment David thought he was going to hit him. Instead he walked out without saying another word. David could hear him on the phone to his father. He stayed where he was, letting the disaster continue to unfold, knowing that Grant was on the other side of the door if he tried to leave.

In a few minutes he heard another truck pulling into the yard and the front door opening, the screen door clanging against the side of the house. No words passed between the two men and then his father was there, looming above where he lay crouched miserably in the tub. His father leaned down and cuffed him hard on the ear, the other side of his head hitting sharply against the tub. Without needing to be told David got up and followed him out, past Grant whose eyes he could not meet, and then home, neither of them speaking.

He did not set foot again in the house, or even the yard, until his return home from college. His father never spoke of the incident that day or after, but the ordeal so scarred David, the exposure of something so his own to the light of day too much to bear, that he refused to put himself in a position where it might be revealed again. The only consequence of that day was his father's insistence from that day forward that his sons would have to leave the farm and town for college or university. If either wanted to return after they had seen something of the wider world they were welcome to, but they would have to stay apart from the place for a time first.

This was no burden for Eric, who David was certain had been plotting his exile since their mother's death. He went to Edmonton and immersed himself in his studies, how stars worked, as he explained it to them. David went more reluctantly, but he knew that this father would not be dissuaded in this matter, and spent two years in Olds taking an agriculture management certificate. That done his father agreed that he could come back and work on the farm. You can live on the Faulkenbourg Place, he told him, and it will give you a place of your own, though David knew that his father only wanted to ensure that his home remained his own.

There was no small irony in his living in the house where the farm hand had lived, for that was in essence what he was in those first years. He and his father were still uneasy around each other, though they had always been so since the time of his mother's illness. His father ran the farm in the same way he always had, keeping his own counsel. David was expected to do the chores first thing in the morning and then stop by the house or shop, wherever his father happened to be, and receive his day's instructions.

David did not mind this arrangement at all, happy simply to be home and at the Faulkenbourg Place, his mind restful for the first time in years. He worked without complaint and in the evenings and weekends would curl or play hockey or baseball, depending on the season. He became a fixture at community social events and was friendly with everyone, so unlike his father in that respect, as everyone said. The time passed easily for him, for this was all he had ever imagined for himself when he had dreamed of the future, living within those walls, the days going as they would.

One night, after some curling, he stopped in at the hotel for a drink and found himself talking with two old timers, Fred Daismith and Jack Kettle.

"You old enough to be in here?" Fred said with a laugh as he sat down, while Jack bought him a beer.

"Never stopped me before," he said.

Both men laughed and began to reminisce about their first beer at the Hotel, which they had shared with his father, after a hardball tournament. They had all been underage, but the rest of the team had insisted they drink with them.

"Pleasant Porter bought that first round as I recall."

"Yes, he did didn't he."

Seeing the confusion on David's face, Fred said, "Your father never told you about Pleasant?"

"He was an older gent who came over to homestead in the late twenties," Jack said. "Always good for a gab."

"Really nice fellow."

"Surprised your dad hadn't mentioned him," Jack said. "We all spent quite a bit of time with him. Curling and playing cards. Until the accident."

David raised his eyebrow in question and Fred shook his head. "Kerosene explosion at his place. Killed him of course. Burned the whole place down. Seems like it was an accident, but I remember there was talk."

"There was talk," Jack said. "Dad always said Louie Glazer had something to do with it."

"People were always saying that back then. I know your dad didn't like him at all," Fred said to David.

"Never heard of him either," David said.

"He had the Faulkenbourg Place after Albert."

Hearing this David went still, tilting his head in, not wanting to miss a word of what was said next.

"He seemed fine enough to me," Jack said. "Little older than us I would guess, though he didn't seem to age a day when he was here."

"All the girls back then definitely had eyes for him. So you know there was talk about that of course. And he always had nice new clothes, looking the part, right. But the quarter was a mess."

"There was talk the one year that he didn't put in a crop until the end of June," Jack said. David could well imagine what his father would think of that.

"Yes that was the problem I suppose. He always had time for girls and cards and the like, never seemed to lack for money – and this was the thirties remember – and never put in a day's work even when he should have."

"What happened to him?" David asked, surprising himself at the need that sounded in his voice.

"That's a strange thing too. Just disappeared. No one knows what happened to him, where he went. Special Areas took the quarter over and sold it once he was declared dead."

Hearing this David felt a shiver of recognition pass through him, as though he had always known of Louie

Glazer and what had befallen him. When he returned home that night it was to walk around a house made anew by this knowledge, running his hands against the walls as though he might touch this long vanished man. The house offered nothing, immutable, its secrets its own both that night and the years that followed.

They were good years though, with grain prices high and the crops good. Soon everyone around town had new trucks and the fields were full of new equipment. After five years, and much success, his father called him over one evening after supper and poured them both a drink.

"We need to talk about your future," he said to David. "Are you serious about staying on?"

"Of course," David said. It felt as though he had just completed an apprenticeship and now was being inducted into a higher order of the guild.

"Then I think you should have some land to your name. The Mernicks told me they're retiring. I think we should put a bid in on their land and put it in your name. That and the Faulkenbourg Place can be yours, and then we can set things up so that I transfer half our land to you in the next ten years or so."

They talked some more and then settled the agreement with another drink and a handshake. David left floating on the air back to the Faulkenbourg Place, which now and truly was his home. That night, unable to sleep with the excitement that was stirring within him, he walked from room to room touching the walls and letting the sensation wash over him.

In the years that followed he began to discover more of the brief and strange existence of Louie Glazer in their town. Few remembered much of him, for he had only lived in the area for six years. From what David could glean from his conversations with those who did recall him, he was a friendly, ingratiating fellow who wormed his way into the confidence of many. Despite that, he had a reputation as someone who was a little disreputable, which only increased his popularity in certain circles. It also explained his father's aversion to the man. David had mentioned Glazer once in passing and his father had responded with a stern look and a shake of his head.

More concerning than his father's opinions on the matter were the deaths that followed Glazer, stalking the friends he ran with in those days. There was Pleasant Porter, of course, and Nels Sletkolem, another bachelor homesteader, who was found dead, his house in flames, the day after he had sold some cattle at the market. And there was Johnny Jones, a young Welshman, who was found dead in his hotel room, where he'd stayed the night celebrating after selling his wheat that fall.

The connection between them all and Glazer seemed to be a card game that Nels had held every week. All had been frequent attendees according to his father's friend, Frank Hardwell. Louie, it was said, would supply the booze for the gatherings, prohibition still being in force in those days. Still, the deaths seemed to be more a terrible confluence of mishaps rather than anything sinister. It was only Jack Kettle's words to him about Pleasant Porter's death that led him to think otherwise. He dismissed such thoughts for the most part though, going about his days.

Some of the old timers in the area had founded a museum in town to chronicle the vanished homesteading life. David's father had donated a rusted out threshing machine that had sat in a field just off the home quarter for some twenty odd years. He had David bring it into town and help Frank Hardwell and Jack Kettle get it up and running again. It was an enjoyable day with a lot of talk of the old days, Frank and Jack telling him stories of his father, a man who in their telling was almost unrecognizable to his son.

They had lunch in the museum office, which had once been the railway agent's home. Now it would house the town archives, including copies of the old newspaper, The

Times. Claire Hillard, a new teacher from Strathmore, was helping to organize them and David sat with her while he had his sandwiches.

"Not the most exciting way to spend your Saturday," he said to her.

She shook her head, "Oh, no, I find it just fascinating, all these old stories."

"I find it hard to believe much interesting ever happened around here."

"Just look at this one," she passed him a yellowed paper that looked as though it might crumble at his touch.

It was about the town treasurer, a William Harris, who had hanged himself after an audit of the records showed he had been skimming funds from the municipality. The article noted that none of the money was recovered from the man's house or from any accounts he might have had. He raised an eyebrow and looked at her.

"See," she said, "Interesting things do happen here."

"Well, strange things anyway I guess."

He was about to hand the article back to her when a name caught his eye at the end of the article. The person who had discovered William Harris' body was Louie Glazer. His blood felt his blood go cold at the sight of it. It was as though the other deaths came into a new focus with that one off-hand sentence. Under this new light it seemed to him there lay a pattern, not mere coincidence, there were too many dead men and too much missing money for this to all be passed off to coincidence.

He saw that Claire was staring at him and realized he had been lost in his thoughts while he stared at the newspaper. He passed it back to her and she smiled. "You look like you've seen a ghost."

He laughed, "Maybe so. The fellow who found the body there, he used to live in the place I'm in right now. Just up and disappeared one day, never been seen since."

"Now that's pretty interesting too, wouldn't you say? And you thought this was a boring old town."

189

"Maybe I was hoping it was," he said.

What remained of the mystery of Louie Glazer would, he knew, be found in the house, if it could be discovered. In the days that followed his epiphany he found himself unable to sleep and took to wandering from the kitchen, to the porch, to the living room and back again. In those hours he often felt as though he inhabited a dream world, that if he stepped outside the house he would find himself transported to some other realm of existence. Maybe in that place, whatever it was, he could find the lost traces of Louie Glazer and satisfy his hunger to know what had happened, but he never dared to leave the house. There he knew comfort.

In the months that followed he started going with Claire and within a year they were married. She moved in with him at the Faulkenbourg Place and almost immediately made plain her dislike of the place. The insulation was very poor, so it was cold throughout the winter, and the stove and fridge were both ancient models. The bathroom had been hastily built the summer his father had restored the house, for the Faulkenbourg's and those who followed had relied on outhouses for their plumbing. These were her stated reasons, but David could sense that his new wife felt uneasy within these walls for reasons she was unable or afraid to express. The pacing of the rooms he sometimes still embarked on those fevered nights when he was unable to sleep went unremarked on, but not unnoticed, he knew.

He promised her their residence would not last long and they settled into a mostly harmonious routine. Two years later Alice was born to the delight of everyone and when two years later Claire was pregnant again his father began to talk about retiring and giving David and his young family the home quarter. They visited the lawyers to have his father's will changed and all seemed set for David to take over the farm in the next year or so.

When his brother got word of the plan he returned home, announcing to both his father and David that he wanted to stay and farm as well. It seemed that his studies had gone poorly, leaving him unsure of what to do and thinking it might be best to return home. Both of them received this announcement in silence, neither of their faces hinting at what they were thinking. His father told Eric he would think about it and the next day when David stopped by the house, a decision had been made.

"You and I got on well enough with the land between us," his father said to him, "So it shouldn't be a problem for the two of you either. It's just a matter of who will get what."

Yes, David thought, yes it is. He said nothing though, for he knew that this was not a matter on which his father would be open for discussion. In due time he would let them know what he considered a fair arrangement for the both of them and they would both have to accept it, for in this he held the keys to the chest.

It galled him, he had to admit, that now, after all these years, Eric was returning. From the moment their mother had fallen ill he had done nothing but plot his escape from the farm, as though it were some prison they had been condemned to. Now, after the years that David had put into building the operation, creating a homestead out of the Faulkenbourg Place and suffering under his father's whims, Eric came back expecting to be given the fruits of others labor as though he was owed it.

These thoughts festered within him in the uneasy days that followed, as the brothers worked together again for the first time in years, awaiting the judgment of their father. Conversation between the two of them was awkward and stilted, the weight of their years apart and the momentous decision to come heavy in both their minds. A few times David noticed Eric watching him when his brother thought he wasn't looking.

He caught him at it one day when they were out

putting up a fence for winter grazing. "Is there something you'd like to say to me?"

Eric shook his head and then a moment later said, "You've changed."

"So have you."

"No," Eric said, slowly, as though thinking it through. "You're different. Like someone else."

David was taken aback, unsure what to say, and they left at that, returning to the posts and the wire. But from that moment on David resolved that his brother would not get the Faulkenbourg Place, whatever secrets lay within it would be his alone. How he could achieve this he could not say, for his father would never relent in his desires, but he would see it done.

Two weeks later their father called them together one evening and told them he had made his decision. The land that was in David's name would stay his and some of the other that was in his own would go to him as well. The other half would go to Eric. The home quarter was to be David's, he had a young family after all. In exchange for that David would give Eric the Faulkenbourg Place so that he might have a home. When he had finished speaking he leaned back in his chair and looked from one brother to other.

It was Eric who spoke first. "Thank you," he said, looking at them both, "I know I have asked a lot of both of you, coming back like I have."

Their father smiled, the first smile of real joy that David had seen in him since their mother had died. "That's why I stayed on, so that you both might have something here when you needed it."

They drank to the agreement and made plans to make the trip to Hanna later that week to settle all the details with the lawyer. That night they were all disturbed in their sleep by a ferocious thunderstorm that lit the sky with lightning for over an hour and brought a torrent of rain and hail. It was very early in the year for such a storm, they had not even started seeding yet. The next morning, as he did the chores, David found one of the bulls they had been planning on turning out with their heifers dead from a lightning strike.

After calling around, he and his father went to the Denton's ranch near the Red Deer River to look at their bulls for a replacement. Mack Denton, as was the custom in these kinds of affairs, took them on a tour of his operation, driving them through several pastures where his cattle were already out, before returning to the main yard where the bulls were. The bulls were at the far end in a pen that connected out to a hillside pasture. Most of them were in drinking water, so Mack left the two of them to look things over while he headed up the hill to bring the others in.

David and his father leaned against the boards of the corral, watching as Mack hollered and drove the rest down towards them. They were both silent, David chewing on a strand of grass, until his father took a lurching step towards him, putting a hand on his shoulder.

"David," he said in a strained voice as he fell into his son's arms.

David cradled him for a moment, looking into his father's eyes, so filled with panic and agony, and then laid him gently on the ground. He knelt beside him for a moment, unable to look away, before jumping to his feet and up the fence, waving and shouting to get Mack's attention.

Though they tried to drive into town to the hospital, they were more than an hour away and his father was dead long before they reached help. The funeral was held two days later and the next week he and Eric, as the executors of the estate went to the lawyers to see to the settling of his affairs. There was little talk, the tension between the two brothers palpable. They returned home in separate trucks, David to the Faulkenbourg Place and Eric to the main yard and the home that was now David's.

That evening Eric stopped by the house and Claire left the brothers alone, taking Alice to one of the neighbors. David poured them both some rye and they sat across from each other at the kitchen table, the windows open to let in the cool night air. Outside the coyotes and foxes began their nightly chorus.

They drank in silence for a time, both unsure where to begin. David started, "I'm not giving you the land. It isn't yours."

Eric shook his head. "You know what Dad wanted."

"I'll sell it to you. For something that's fair. I'm not selling the Faulkenbourg Place though."

"What about the home quarter then."

"I'm keeping that too."

"Why would you need both?" David shrugged. "So I'm supposed to buy the land off you and then I have to set up my own place as well."

"It's not like you were here to set up this one."

Eric looked stunned. "Is that what this is really about? That I didn't come home. You know why I didn't. For a long time I thought I wouldn't, but when Dad said he was ready to retire I just realized that this is where I want to be."

David was silent, sipping his drink, staring past his brother.

"To be honest," Eric said, "I imagined us doing this together."

"Look, with the money Dad had for you, you can get a line of credit from the bank and I can sell you your half of the land," David said. "I'll give you a fair price. More than fair. Since I'm keeping the Faulkenbourg Place I'll give you Walker's instead. It's better land anyway."

Eric shook his head. "I don't even know who I'm talking to here. Do you know what this means? If you do this, when I walk out this door tonight, our relationship is done. That's it."

"I know," David said, getting up to refresh their drinks. "I know what this means. It doesn't have to be. I'm willing to be fair about this. But I understand if you don't feel that way."

"Fair? Dad was giving you the land. And you're selling it to me."

"I worked here for ten years. It was as much mine as it was his. And until you came back it would have been all mine. But I don't mind giving it up, I just think I should be paid a little for it."

"You know what Dad wanted."

"I know what he wanted, and I would have gone along with it, even if I didn't necessarily agree with it."

"Lucky for you then."

David was taken aback. "What do you mean?"

Eric leaned across the table so that he could stare directly into his brother's eyes. "I talked to Mack Denton."

"About what?"

"I know what happened."

David stood up, "What the hell did Mack tell you?"

"Sit down," Eric said, standing as well. David did not move, his eyes on his brother's hands which were curled into fists.

Eric exhaled, the tension loosening in his arms and he said, "Mack told me what happened. You were both by the pen and then you jumped at Dad and he fell. He couldn't really see what you were doing but he thought it looked funny. And by the time he got there Dad was basically dead."

"Eric," David said, "He was falling. He was having a heart attack and falling, so I caught him."

"Was he? How close did McKracken look at him? We'll never know now he's in the ground."

"Jesus Eric," David said, "Listen to yourself."

"No, you listen," Eric said and slammed his fist on the table, toppling the bottle of rye. "You listen. You did this. This is the only way you could get everything you wanted and you got it."

David was so astonished he could not even summon a response and Eric, still furious, stormed out of the house. David could hear the slam of his truck door and the engine starting. There was a long pause, the engine idling, before he heard the truck being shifted into gear and then another before Eric headed down the driveway and disappeared down the road. Only then did David move, rousing himself from his stupor, to right the bottle of rye. He poured himself another and wandered from room to room taking the feel of the house in.

Walter was born that November, a month after they had moved into the house on the home quarter. Eric returned to Edmonton, reconciling with the girl he had been seeing, and taking up his life there anew. David viewed this with some satisfaction, the universe restoring itself to equilibrium. Claire had stayed out of the brothers' dispute, making no comment when Eric left and they moved into the home quarter except to say, "You have to fix this. You'll never forgive yourself."

David had not replied and had done nothing. As far as he was concerned, Eric was the one who needed to make a gesture of reconciliation after what he had said that last night. He hadn't dedicated himself to this world, sacrificed what David had sacrificed, he had simply arrived thinking he could take what was there. The only other fallout from his father's death, and the fracture in his relationship with Eric, was the talk that now followed him around town, folks looking at him sideways out of the corner of their eyes. The man who had stolen his father's farm, was what was said, though after a time such talk died down as those of his father's generation retired and passed on.

The farm itself continued to prosper and expand under David's guidance. When Jack Kettle decided to retire David bought his pasture land and added another fifty head of cattle to his operation. With the workload growing, and without his father to support him, David had to bring on a farm hand. To the surprise of his neighbors and everyone in town, the man, and those who followed him, were not set up in the Faulkenbourg Place as would have been logical. They rented a place in town or later stayed in a trailer David bought and set up in the main yard.

When asked about this oddity David would shrug and say that people didn't like staying in the Faulkenbourg Place. It was small, cold in the winter and, especially as the years went on, old and outdated. People shook their heads and talked about this, another mark on his character to go with the unpleasantness that had come out of his father's death. But as time went by the abnormality of it simply became what he was and was not commented on, except by those who found reason to be outraged by the flagrant waste of a perfectly good house. It will go to ruin they said, with nobody staying in it and nobody keeping it up.

The house did not though, remaining stalwart against the elements, the dry windswept heat of the summers and the frigid snow-ridden winters. David too passed the years well, hardly seeming to age a day in ten years. He would still return to the Faulkenbourg Place when he was unable to sleep, pacing from room to room in the darkness as he had done so many times before. For a time there was a purpose to his wandering, as he rapped against each wall and ran his finger along every seam, looking for a place where Louie Glazer might have hidden whatever secrets and money he possessed.

He found no trace of anything, not of money, nor of Glazer himself. The house remained a harbor for his soul, his existence tied to it in some inextricable yet inexpressible way. Even as he got older and more reflective, watching his children grow up and wondering at the fundamental strangeness of all their beings, he never questioned that he should more linked to this house than his children or his wife. That was how it had always been, and he presumed it would remain so.

One day, driving by the house on his way back from town, he thought he spotted a flash of movement from one of the windows. Thinking it might be some high school kids using it for an afternoon of drinking, he turned his truck around and drove back. He found a man sitting at the kitchen table, as though he had been expecting him. He was well-turned out in a brown suit, his hair shining and combed back on his head, a newsboy cap overturned on the table before him. He looked familiar to David, almost recognizable, though he could not for the life of him recall where their paths might have crossed before.

The man didn't say anything, but gestured for David to sit, which he did, studying the other's face intently. He was younger than David, though he dressed as though he were much older, with his suit and his hat. He had dark eyes and hair and a mouth that set in a smile. He reached into his shirt pocket and pulled out a toothpick which he began to twirl and chew on as he studied David.

"What are you doing here?" David asked when it became evident the man was waiting for him to speak.

"I might ask the same of you."

David looked the man over again. "It's my house. I own it."

The man shook his head. "It's been mine for some time now."

"The bank says differently, I'm afraid."

The man removed the toothpick from his mouth, flashing his lips into a deeper grin. "Papers mean nothing. You should know that."

David shook his head not knowing what to say. "What we have here," the man said, tapping at the table with his fist, "Goes deeper than any of that."

He gestured at the world outside the house and David felt the breath go still in his chest. He looked at the man's clothes again; the sharply pressed suit looked new, though the style was forty years old. Maybe older, certainly before

David's time. There was, he realized, no doubt who this man could be.

"What do we do about this then?" he asked.

The man smiled, flicking the toothpick to the other side of his mouth. "There are two sisters: one gives birth to the other and she, in turn, gives birth to the first. Who are they?"

David closed his eyes and tried to steady his breath. A part of him wanted to get up and walk out, turn from these shadows to the light of day and never return. The moment to do so was now, he knew, for after this there could be no turning back. He understood this in the same instinctive and deep-rooted way that he had always understood just what the house was and why this man was now here. The danger was obvious: he stood upon a precipice where any wrong step could lead to a fall. Yet he did not leave, it was not in him to, he would not surrender this place to another.

His mind seemed to be a vast sea of nothingness as he pondered what the man had said, the harder he tried to pull some word from those depths the more absolute the vacuum became. At last he swallowed. "Night and Day."

He was rewarded with a nod from the man. Cursing the fact that he had never been much interested in books or school to have learned any riddles, he tried to piece something together. The man looked at him without expression, saying nothing, as though he had all the time in existence.

"The more you take, the more you leave behind."

"Footsteps," was the man's answer, said almost before David had finished speaking. "Not a king. Not a priest. But dresses for a feast."

He could feel sweat on his forehead and running down his back, his mouth dry. "A clothesline," he said.

Thinking back to a book that his brother had pressed upon him, some silly thing about elves and dragons, he said, "It devours any living thing, turns stone to dust, eats at metal, and ruins anything that man can build."

The man considered this, rolling the toothpick in his between his fingers, before pulling it out of his mouth. "Time," he said and smiled. "The tower is high, higher than any tower in this world. Nonetheless, it has no shade."

David repeated the words in his head and then did so again. Though he knew he didn't have the answer he still strove to find some lost corner of his mind, some thought that would unlock the riddle. What could be so tall but cast no shade? The man's smile broadened as victory appeared in his grasp and David felt tears come into the corner of his eyes and his face go hot and flush.

He said nothing, dropping his head and slumping in defeat, and at last the man stood and put on his cap. He walked by David, placing a hand on his shoulder as he did, and went out the door.

IF YOU ENJOYED
ON THE FAR HORIZON,
YOU MIGHT ALSO LIKE:

THE DEVIOUS KIND

The body of a local woman is found in a coulee on a ranch north of Loverna, her head blown off with a shotgun. New to town and the job, Constable Martin Thomas arrives on the scene as a spring snowstorm begins to wipe out all evidence before his investigation has even begun.

There is no shortage of suspects to consider. A spurned husband. A jealous lover. A betrayed business partner. And family members battling over an inheritance. All have motive and opportunity. And no one seems to be telling him everything.

As he tries to sift the truth from the lies, the snowstorm continues to build, leaving Loverna cut off from the outside world. And Thomas alone to face a killer who will do anything not to get caught.

1

The body lay, sprawled awkwardly, partway down the coulee, right before the slope turned sheer and plunged to the creek far below. The night had hidden it, but the arrival of dawn made its presence obvious. There were several sets of footprints from where the body lay to the road, clearly marked in the muddy spring ground. Even as the new day's light revealed these details, the first flakes of snow began to fall, wet and heavy. For a time the earth resisted their intrusion, but eventually the storm proved too much and the ground turned white, covering over the tracks.

Wayne Johnstone noticed the body later that morning. By then the snow had covered all but the person's red jacket, which stood out vividly against the backdrop of white snow and the drab browns and greys of late March on the Canadian prairies. There was no green yet anywhere, not even any buds on the trees, spring only tentatively taking hold. The arrival of the storm promised that winter would not yet go quietly.

Even still he almost missed it, distracted by his worry about the storm's arrival. He had one hundred fifty cows still to calve and they were coming in bunches now. If the storm was as big as promised—and it looked to be, the snow descending so thickly he sometimes had trouble making out the highway—then he would likely lose some calves today.

There was little he could do about it, but it still worked at his thoughts, as he drove the tractor into the far pen where he turned out the cows who had already calved. Many were already tucked into the slat-fenced shelter near the gate, but they followed him deeper into the pen, heads low against the snow, waiting for the feed to emerge from the tub grinder.

It was as he reached the end of the first row of feed, and turned the tractor around to start the second, that he caught sight of the red jacket. Thinking it was something that had come off a passing car, he drove to the edge of the pen by the lip of the slope to see what it might be. Something in him recognized just what and who it was immediately, and he sat in the tractor, his hands clutching the steering wheel, feeling very cold.

After a time he clambered down the hillside, now slick with the accumulating snow, to confirm his suspicions. He stood looking down at her, the snow gathering on his shoulders and hat, before he managed to gather himself and return to the tractor. He reached into his pocket for his cell phone to call Diane, but stopped himself. Somehow it didn't seem right announcing this to her over the phone. He got back into the tractor and finished up with the last row for the cattle, before returning to the house.

He left the tractor running and went inside. Diane was in the kitchen lingering over her last cup of coffee. He called her from the entryway and she ducked her head around the corner to look at him, a frown on her face, knowing there had to be something wrong for him to have come in so soon after leaving.

"I just found Kristi Taid's body in the coulee," he said after a moment's hesitation. Saying the words made it feel much more real.

Diane seemed to not understand. "What's she doing out there?"

"She's dead," Wayne said with a heavy sigh. "Shotgun to the head."

"Oh," Diane said, reflecting and staring off glassy-eyed into the distance. "Better call the police, I guess."

Wayne was already fishing into his pocket to remove his cell phone. "Do you have the number?"

"Well, just 911, right? This has to be an emergency. My God, poor Leonard. I wonder if Clarissa's home."

Wayne nodded, realizing he had never in his life called the emergency line before. He stared at the flip phone in his hands, pulling it open gingerly, still unsure of the device. Diane had insisted he get one in case of emergencies, but the phone did not feel comfortable in his hands. Using it was still not intuitive. Briefly, he found himself wondering if he needed to dial a different emergency number for cell phones only, before dismissing that as ridiculous. Now he dialed and waited, listening to the ring.

"I'm going to call Leonard," Diane said.

"Don't," Wayne said, as the operator began to speak. "The police won't like that."

"I have to," Diane said.

Wayne knew better than to argue. He talked with the operator, telling what he had seen, and was told the constable would be on his way shortly. The detachment was in Loverna, Wayne knew, half an hour away. Probably more in the snow. He had time enough to get a few of the chores done before this new storm descended upon him, and he headed out the door to do so.

2

Half an hour later, a police car drove slowly up the driveway into the main yard, pulling to a stop in front of the ranch house, where Diane stood on the porch, a dog at her feet and a hood thrown over her head to keep off the snow.

"Hello, Diane," Constable Martin Tomas said as he stepped out of the car.

She just nodded. "It's down there by the coulee," she said, pointing. "You can take your car if you think it can make it through the mud."

"I'll be all right."

She paused, and then said, "We called him. Wayne said I probably shouldn't, but I had to."

He nodded. "He's down there now?"

"Yeah."

Martin got back into his car and drove slowly down the laneway that led to the far pens that edged onto the coulee. He went past pens filled with cattle still heavy with their winter coats, but he paid them no mind. Even six months ago he might have, but now, a year and a half into his term here, a cow was just a cow.

He arrived at the gate to the far corral, and could see Wayne's truck, a brand new 2003 Dodge Ram, parked by the fence and, on the other side, two figures staring down at the ground. Martin knew what they were looking at. He debated driving his car through the pen, but decided it was a poor idea. The ground would be soft in there, and the last thing he needed on a day like this was to get stuck in a corral.

It would have been easier, he realized, peering through the snow, if he had gone out to the highway and parked there, coming down through the ditch to the coulee. That was likely what had happened with whoever had killed Kristi Taid. With that thought, he reversed course and went out to the highway, parking his car on the shoulder and putting his hazards on, hoping that anyone who happened down the road would be able to see enough to spot them.

He stepped and slid his way from the road down into the ditch and from there made his way gingerly down the incline toward the coulee. A fence ran along the highway, ending at the coulee's edge, and Martin found himself wondering why Wayne hadn't bothered to extend it further. The coulee was part of his land and there was a pasture down below, but likely there was a fence somewhere there to keep the cattle from it.

Not that the cattle would be likely to ever make there way from the ravine's bottom up the highway. Even from its edge, Martin could not make out the coulee's bottom, could not see the creek that twisted and wound its way through its narrow passes. Trees, short and narrow-trunked, like all prairie trees, lined either side, obscuring what lay within.

The two men, both with lean rancher's frames made bulky by the winter clothes they were wearing, were watching as he approached. Martin could not make out their expressions through the swirl of the snow falling, for which he was oddly glad. He set his shoulders and nodded at them.

"Hello, Martin. Thanks for coming," Wayne said. He was a tall man, and would have been gangly in his youth.

Age had thickened him somewhat and now, in his early sixties, he appeared as a solid presence beside the more sleight Leonard, still powerful, in spite of his age.

"No problem," Martin said, an automatic reply, which sounded stupid, given the situation.

The other man, hood up on his jacket, hunched over to better keep his face clear of snow, did not say anything. His eyes had not strayed from the ground where the body lay. Martin looked at him carefully, now that he was up close, but his expression was blank. He seemed not to even realize that someone else had arrived on the scene. Well, it was his wife on the ground, after all.

Wayne moved aside so that Martin could get near the body. Martin stepped in, smiling his thanks and crouched over the body. The face was mostly blown away. He could see the outline of one eye socket and most of the jaw, bits of brain and skull. Her neck and chest were perforated with pellet blasts. The blood was that curdled dark color, clumping against her skin and the earth below. He sighed and stood up, turning to Leonard.

"It's her, all right," Leonard said. "That's her jacket and shoes."

Martin looked at Wayne. "Anybody else been down here but you two?"

Wayne shook his head.

"All right. Why don't you and Leonard head back to the house and wait for me? I want to look around a bit. Cory should be here pretty quick."

"What'll they do with the body?" Leonard asked, his tone odd.

"He'll have to take it into town. Botha will have to look at it. We'll take care of it."

He turned and knelt again by the body. The two others remained where they were, as though unsure of whether they should in fact leave, before Wayne reached out and put an arm on Leonard's shoulder and led him back to the pen. Martin looked up from the body, not leaving his crouch, and watched them get into Wayne's truck and drive back through the corral, the tires leaving clear tracks in the snow.

An eerie quiet descended around him, a product of the stillness that seemed to always come with a snowfall. The only sounds that intruded on his study of the body were the wind cutting through the coulee and the odd cow calling out to a calf in the pen beside him. He could hear his own breathing, which sounded hushed, as if even he did not want to disturb this scene.

It had already been disturbed, though; the snow had seen to that. The body had been dragged here, likely from the highway, given the lack of blood surrounding her and the severity of the gunshot wounds. The snow had already obscured any evidence of that passage, as well as the footprints of whoever had carried her here. There was also the matter of the remainder of her head, which was no doubt in pieces wherever she had been shot.

Where had she been shot and why had she been brought here? He stood up and found himself looking in the direction of the Taid's ranch. It did not make sense that Leonard would bring her here if he wanted to direct attention away from himself, given his home was only a mile away. And if someone else were trying to point the finger in his direction, they would be more likely to make sure her body was found somewhere on his land.

This felt more like an idea that had occurred in passing as the killers rushed to hide the trail that led to them. Dump the body in the coulee and hope the storm, which everyone had known was coming, would hide the body. If they had gotten her farther down into the coulee it very well might have, Martin realized. And if the coyotes had gotten to the body, it might have been a very long time indeed before any trace was found of her.

Which led to another question: why here? Why not take the body down farther and deeper into the trees? The body lay between two short, shrub-like trees, but without their leaves the body was exposed to both the road and the pen. Whoever had done it was in a rush, working in the dark so that Wayne and Diane didn't chance to see them, perhaps struggling with weight of the corpse. They had come this far and judged it far enough. What had led to that haste, and where had they been going initially before they changed their plans and chose this place to hide the body?

He paced from the body back to the road. The only tracks leading into the ditch were his own, and even they were rapidly disappearing. He climbed back up onto the highway, kicking at the damp blacktop. Soon it too would surrender to the snow, disappearing beneath it. The road curved just ahead along with the coulee, the two running nearly parallel briefly, before it curved again to wrap around the valley. The snow was coming down so heavily he could not see beyond that.

He went back to the body, snapping on the rubber gloves he had brought as he went, feeling faintly ridiculous as he did so. This was his first murder investigation, and he was very conscious of making a misstep and also of being found out for a fraud. That, as much as anything else, had been why he sent Wayne and Leonard away. Though obviously Leonard was very much a suspect, Martin could not have both of them around further contaminating the crime scene.

All he knew about conducting this sort of investigation he had learned at the academy in Regina, though the principles were the same as with any of the dozens of robberies and assaults he had been called in on while here or in Wetaskawin, where he had been stationed previously. It did not feel that way now that he was faced with a dead body. This felt of much greater import. A life had been lost, after all. And it fell to him to determine who had been responsible.

Wiping his eyes clear of water and snow, he knelt down and gingerly turned what was left of Kristi's head toward him and pulled back her remaining eyelid. The eye beneath was cloudy and the body itself stiff with rigor mortis, no doubt helped by the temperature, which had hovered around the freezing mark for most of the night through to the morning.

Martin stood, clicking his tongue against the roof of his mouth thoughtfully, and started to pull his gloves off when he heard a vehicle approaching. He watched as the ambulance pulled up behind his car and Cory slid his bulk out from behind the wheel. The ambulance driver wandered over, his jeans tucked into unlaced work boots, his jacket open to the elements as well. He was unshaven and, as he came up alongside, Martin caught a whiff of booze.

"Late night?"

"Oh," Cory said with a wave of his hand. His eyes were bloodshot, but that was hardly surprising for Cory. In spite of the fact they were both in their early thirties, Martin always thought of Cory as being much younger. He certainly acted like it.

"You good to drive yet?"

"I made it here, didn't I?"

"Don't make me put the fucking Breathalyzer on you," Martin said. "I've got enough shit to deal with without you cocking things up."

Cory waved his hand again and turned his attention to the body. "Kristi Taid."

"Yes," Martin said.

"Cause of death shouldn't be a problem, anyway."

"No."

"Well, how you wanna do this? Bring the stretcher down from the highway, probably the easiest."

Martin agreed, and they both made their way up the ditch to the back of the ambulance, where they offloaded the stretcher. Together they wheeled it down into the ditch and gingerly set Kristi's body upon it. Beneath where her body had lain was only dormant grass and dead leaves. No doubt he was ruining all kinds of forensic evidence, but who knew how long it would take for the RCMP to send a forensics team out. The storm would only complicate things further, and Martin could not just leave the body here for all the world driving by to see.

Once the body was safely strapped to the stretcher, they wheeled it back up the ditch, both of them slipping and cursing on the slope. When they had the stretcher safely into the back of the ambulance, Cory turned to Martin.

"Take it in to Botha, then?"

"Yes," Martin said. "And for fuck's sake, Cory, don't phone anyone, don't let anyone know. This is an RCMP investigation now."

Cory didn't reply, giving him another wave, and was on his way. Martin sighed and swore again under his breath. He stood and watched until the ambulance had disappeared in the snow. He waited before getting into his own car, looking up at the vast wall of grey clouds above him, already thinking of the questions he would have to ask Leonard.

THE DEVIOUS KIND is now available.

ABOUT THE AUTHOR

Clint Westgard writes mystery, crime and western novels, as well as science fiction and fantasy. He has published a work of historical fantasy set in colonial Peru, The Maleficio Chronicles, and a retelling of the Minotaur legend, The Trials of the Minotaur. He lives in Calgary, Alberta.

ALSO BY CLINT WESTGARD

The Devious Kind

A Mystery

The body of a local woman is found in a coulee on a ranch north of Loverna, her head blown off with a shotgun. New to town and the job, Constable Martin Thomas arrives on the scene as a spring snowstorm begins to wipe out all evidence before his investigation has even begun.

There is no shortage of suspects to consider. A spurned husband. A jealous lover. A betrayed business partner. And family members battling over an inheritance. All have motive and opportunity. And no one seems to be telling him everything.

As he tries to sift the truth from the lies, the snowstorm continues to build, leaving Loverna cut off from the outside world. And Thomas alone to face a killer who will do anything not to get caught.

ALSO BY CLINT WESTGARD

The Maleficio Chronicles

Luisa is always more than she appears. Rumor and mystery surround her. And strange events seem to follow wherever she goes.

Born in Lima, City of Kings, to a noble family, her father so fears her true nature that he banishes her to a convent. There she falls under the suspicion of the Inquisition and decides to flee.

Disguised as a man, she embarks upon a series of wild adventures, dueling, carousing, and gambling her way across colonial Peru. But everything changes when someone recognizes her for what she truly is, and soon she finds herself fighting for her very survival.

In a world where she will always stand apart, Luisa undergoes a strange journey, marked by betrayal and murder, terrible powers and mysterious strangers. *The Maleficio Chronicles* is her incredible confession and a story like no other.

ALSO BY CLINT WESTGARD

The Trials of the Minotaur

In the fifth year of the rule of Auten the One Eyed a
minotaur is born to one of Colosi's most important
families.

Taken from his mother as a newborn, exiled and cast from
his family, the minotaur vows to return to the imperial city
and take his rightful place as a patrician in the empire. But
the patriarch of the family, his grandfather, will stop at
nothing to see this blemish to his honor destroyed.

And so begins an epic journey, through lands beyond
imagining, marked by despair and exile, triumph and
betrayal. At its heart lies a quest to be free.

ALSO BY CLINT WESTGARD

The Forgotten
Volume One of The Sojourners Cycle

Who is David Aeida? And what does he know that has so
many people pursuing him?

David doesn't know. He can't remember anything about
who he is. But he finds himself ensnared in a vicious
conflict between a religious cult and a guild that patrols the
crossings between multiple universes. They will both stop
at nothing to gain whatever knowledge he possesses. Most
dangerous of all, is the implacable hunter, known only as
the Seeker, who has his own reasons for wanting to find
David.

His only hope is to recover his memories before they do.
His only ally is a woman named Meredith, and she
definitely knows more than she is telling...

Spanning both universes and the human mind, The
Forgotten is an unforgettable science fiction thriller that
questions the very nature of identity. It is the first volume
of the Sojourners Cycle, an epic that will encompass the
fates of universes and humanity itself.

ALSO BY CLINT WESTGARD

The Apostate
Volume Two of The Sojourners Cycle

Laila has only one goal in mind. To have her revenge upon
the Grand Regent for all he has done to her. First, though,
she needs to find her way across the universes.

That is easier said than done. The Grand Regent's agents
are still pursuing her. As is the Society of Travellers. And
the Seeker lurks somewhere, waiting for his moment to
strike.

Laila has a plan, though, and a few tricks of her own. But
she will discover that not everything is at seems. For the
war she has given her life to hides a far greater conflict.

Spanning multiple universes and the complexities of the
human mind, The Apostate, continues the incredible
journey begun in The Forgotten. The second volume of
The Sojourners Cycle is an unforgettable science fiction
epic that encompasses the fates of universes and humanity
itself.

ALSO BY CLINT WESTGARD

The Acolyte
Volume Three of The Sojourners Cycle

After crossing the universes to join with Toma Osahi's
group of renegades in their battle for control of the
Church of Regents, Laila finds herself in a precarious
position. While they both share the same goal—the
destruction of the Grand Regent—Osahi doesn't know
who Laila really is. What will he do if he finds out?

While Laila struggles to keep her identity secret, Osahi and
his people pull her deeper and deeper into a search for
Ana that promises to shed light on the dark secrets of the
Watchers' Order and the Acolytes. Before she can find
those answers though, Laila will have to face what lies
within.

Crossing the universes has unsettled the already shaky
equilibrium in her mind. If she wants to return herself to
her own body, she will have to act fast, for the
consequences of what Acolytes did to her are still
reverberating. And Aeida hides somewhere, waiting for his
time to come.

The thrilling third volume of the Sojourners Cycle
continues Laila's incredible journey across the universes
against incredible odds, as well as exploring her past,
including the pivotal role she played in the rise of the
Grand Regent and her own downfall at his hands.

ALSO BY CLINT WESTGARD

The Double
Volume Four of The Sojourners Cycle

David Aeida now commands his body, having cast Laila
aside. He has sworn fealty to the Grand Regent, who
wants him by his side and sees that his loyalty is rewarded.

But the Grand Regent is not the man he was. He is
paranoid and suspicious of everyone, isolated in his tower,
and thirsting for vengeance against those he feels have
wronged him. How long until he turns on Aeida as well?

That is only the beginning of Aeida's problems. For he
knows the Seeker and the Society of Travelers remain to
play their parts. Both desire nothing more than the utter
destruction of the Church of Regents and all its works.
And though Laila has been defeated, he knows better than
anyone not to assume she has been vanquished.

The epic fourth volume of the Sojourners Cycle centers
upon the many betrayals and lies at the heart of the faith of
the Church of Regents and the devastation upon the lives
of the faithful they have wrought. Desire and guilt, love
and revenge, rage and despair will drive them all, with
consequences for all the universes.

ALSO BY CLINT WESTGARD

The Sojourner
Volume Five of The Sojourners Cycle

Laila's strange and reluctant alliance with the Seeker continues, though she does not know where it will lead her. She fears it will place her in another prison, worse than the one she has just managed to escape.

But her escape is not entirely complete. For though she has been restored to her own flesh, parts of Aeida somehow still remain. Along with some other she does not recognize. Is this some aftereffect of the Acolyte's bizarre procedure? Or the result of the Seeker's meddling?

All this pales in comparison to what Laila soon discovers. That she has an unwanted part to play in an ancient struggle for who will rule the crossings between the universes and all that lies in them.

In the stunning conclusion to the Sojourners Cycle Laila will be faced with a terrible choice, one that will decide her fate and humanity's.

ALSO BY CLINT WESTGARD

Realm of Shadows
Volume One of The Shadow Men

Craitol and Renuih, two empires a world apart, divided by
the desert that lies between them. A desert ruled by the
Shadow Men.

An uneasy peace holds sway in both realms, hiding
longstanding feuds and bitter rivalries. Until a Shadow
Men raid on Renuih shatters the calm and sets in motion
events no one can control.

Masiph id Ezern, unfavored son of the Imperial Vazeir,
finds himself a hero following the raid. His father remains
unmoved by his exploits and, in his bitterness, Masiph will
find himself a reluctant participant in a plot against the
empire.

As he finds himself drawn deeper and deeper into the
conspiracy, he soon realizes there will be no escaping the
realm of shadows, where intrigue and betrayal abound.
And though the Shadow Men have gone quiet, they will
not stay silent forever…

ALSO BY CLINT WESTGARD

Council of Shadows
Volume Two of The Shadow Men

Discontent continues to fester within the realms of Craitol and Renuih, fed by intrigues carried out in the shadows. As rivals and apostates struggle for supremacy, a long incubated plan begins to unfold.

Vyissan, a mysterious alkemycal practitioner arrives in Renuih, the latest strike in a long war over who shall control the secrets of alkemya and Craitol itself. He carries with him a secret that, once revealed, will reverberate across all realms. Before he can reveal it though, the conspirators against the emperor will strike their own blow.

But now, a new and more powerful menace looms on the horizon. The Shadow Men have gained the secrets of the Council Adept's alkemya and no one can be certain what they will do with it...

ALSO BY CLINT WESTGARD

Dance of Shadows
Volume Three of The Shadow Men

War with the Shadow Men looms in both realms as the consequences of the Gvers' Council in Craitol begin to make themselves known. A war that could end in glorious triumph or bitter disaster.

Doubt shadows everyone's steps, for they know there are no certainties in the desert. Especially now the Shadow Men have made the art of alkemya their own.

No one has more questions than Vyissan, for he is working in service to a cause he is no longer sure he believes in. And now he must undertake a journey with those who both loathe and fear him. Before the first sword is drawn, his life will be under threat.

But his will not be the only one, for somewhere in the desert the Shadow Men lie in wait.